girl stuff.

ALSO BY LISI HARRISON

The Clique series

Alphas series

FOR OLDER READERS

Monster High series

Pretenders series

girl stuff.

lisi harrison

putnam

G. P. PUTNAM'S SONS

G. P. PUTNAM'S SONS
An imprint of Penguin Random House LLC, New York

Produced by Alloy Entertainment
30 Hudson Yards, 22nd Floor
New York, NY 10001

Visit us online at penguinrandomhouse.com
Library of Congress Cataloging-in-Publication Data
Names: Harrison, Lisi, author.
Title: Girl stuff / Lisi Harrison.
Description: New York: G. P. Putnam's Sons, [2021] | Summary: Seventh graders
Fonda, Drew, and Ruthie develop a friendship strong enough to tackle whatever
middle school—and puberty—throws at them next.
Identifiers: LCCN 2020040059 | ISBN 9781984814982 (trade paperback) |
ISBN 9781984814975 (ebook)
Subjects: CYAC: Friendship—Fiction. | Middle schools—Fiction. | Schools—Fiction.
Classification: LCC PZ7.H2527 Gi 2021 | DDC [Fic]—dc23
LC record available at https://lccn.loc.gov/2020040059

Printed in the United States of America
ISBN 9781984814982
5 7 9 10 8 6 4

Design by Suki Boynton
Text set in Freight Text Pro

This novel is for you, dear reader,
because girl stuff is hard. Be kind to each other
and find the funny in everything.

♥

This is also for Luke and Jesse Harrison
even though they will probably never read it.
(Don't get me started on boy stuff.)

chapter one.

FONDA MILLER GLUED a picture to her vision board and smiled a little. It was a half-staff smile that, if texted, would require two emojis since it felt happy *and* sad at the same time.

In the picture, she and her best friends, Drew Harden and Ruthie Goldman, were lying in a heap on Fonda's front lawn laughing themselves breathless. It had been taken two months earlier, back in June, moments before five heartless parents ripped them apart.

They had been so upset about saying goodbye for the summer that they tied their ankles together in protest. While they were tying, Fonda's mother, Joan, had tried to convince them the eight weeks would fly by. Then Drew's dad chimed in from the driveway next door.

"The separation will be healthy. Especially since you'll be going to the same school when you get back."

"He's right," said Mrs. Harden. "Nesties need breaks every now and then."

Drew rolled her hazel eyes. Probably because she couldn't stand when her mother combined words. "Why can't she say *neighbors* and *besties* like a normal person?" Drew snorted, which made Ruthie and Fonda laugh harder.

And Ruthie's parents, well, they were at work wrapping things up before their family road trip to Washington, DC. But if the Goldmans had been there, they would have said something like *Poplar Creek is beautiful, but there's no culture here and even less diversity. It's important to leave our sunny Southern California bubble and explore the outside world*. That was the kind of thing they always said. Learning was their cardio.

The parents were only trying to help. But their words couldn't fill the pit of loneliness inside Fonda's stomach. They couldn't make long summer days fly by. And they couldn't bike to town for frozen yogurt. They were nothing more than verbal Band-Aids, well-intended distractions that never fully stuck.

So, with their ankles bound together by a worn skipping rope, Fonda, Drew, and Ruthie took big stubborn strides toward the top of their cul-de-sac. *Goodbye, Poplar Creek, and hello, someplace where grown-ups let "nesties" spend summers together. Someplace with free fro-yo and unlimited toppings!*

Then . . . *Thunk.*

Within seconds, they fell out of step with one another and timbered onto Fonda's front lawn, and they were separated the next day.

Now, two months later, Fonda couldn't wait to see them again, and she doubly couldn't wait for them to see her new, ultrasophisticated flat-ironed hair. Only three more sleeps . . .

"Joan, can we stop this now?" asked Winfrey, Fonda's older sister, who had recently started addressing their mother by her first name. The sixteen-year-old was standing over the kitchen table, scissors dangling from her fingers like an old handbag. "I'm getting vision *bored.*"

She had gotten her driver's license earlier that day (third time's a charm!) and thought she was all that. But when a girl has cactus-green eyes, butterscotch-colored highlights, and three number one surf trophies, she kind of is.

"More like vision *blurred*," Amelia said, rubbing her baby blues for effect. At fourteen and a half, she had her own, equally intimidating brand of cool. Tall and lithe, she was a fierce beach volleyball player who managed to pass swimsuits off as clothing, though it was her fiery auburn waves and statement sunglasses that made her a fan favorite.

Then there was Fonda. Petite, flat-chested, and secretly loving the whole back-to-school vision board thing. The paper scraps, Chinese takeout boxes, and glue smells made her insides tingle with delight. Or maybe Fonda was tingling because for the first time all summer, she wasn't feeling her friends' absences the way one feels the hollow churn of stomach upset. She wasn't angling to be included in her sisters' plans or scrolling through Insta, hearting everyone else's #goodtimes while she watched, and rewatched, Netflix original movies. Tonight, the Miller girls were hanging out together. Tonight, Winfrey and Amelia were not calling Fonda a tagalong. Tonight, she was a be-long, just like them.

"Honestly, Joan," Winfrey said, biting into a dumpling. "Why do we have to do this?"

"Vision boards help us identify our goals," Joan said with the patience of someone who hadn't already explained it. *Twice.*

"And why do we need to do *that*?"

"If you can't visualize them, you can't manifest them."

Amelia began tapping the screen of her phone. "There's gotta be an app for this."

"For *what*?"

"Manifesting goals."

Joan swiped the phone from Amelia and stuffed it in the pocket of her overalls. "No screens. Manifest with your hands. It's more rewarding."

"Hey, Amelia, why don't you put a picture of a vision board app on your vision board?" Fonda joked. "That way you'll get one."

No one laughed. Instead, Winfrey gripped her belly and groaned, "Rumble in the jungle. Can I be excused?"

"Same," Amelia said, with a teeny smirk. "I think the moo shu chicken was bad."

They hurried off giggling, leaving behind two anemic vision boards, one with a crooked photo of a tropical beach and the other of surfers hanging out around a bonfire.

Most moms would insist they come back to the table, but Joan, a feminist studies professor at UC Irvine, encouraged freedom of expression, even when the expression didn't deserve to be freed.

"Did you eat bad chicken too?" Joan asked Fonda, offering her an out if she wanted one.

Fonda shook her head. Because, really? What else was she going to do on a Tuesday night? The odd jobs that kept her busy all summer had ended. Which was fine. There were only so many babies to sit, dogs to walk, and hours a girl could spend working at the community pool snack shack before she lost her marbles. But Drew and Ruthie wouldn't be back until Friday, and school didn't start until the following week. So, yeah, Fonda was on board (pun intended).

Besides, her sisters weren't exactly begging Fonda to fake food poisoning with them. As always, they were probably planning to sneak off to a secluded beach or some cute boy's house. And as always, that plan did not include her.

It wasn't that they didn't like her. It was that they didn't have much need for her. In their eyes, Fonda was still a baby. It didn't matter that she had just turned thirteen and was less than two years younger than Amelia. Until Fonda's body made a woman out of her, her sisters would keep saying things like *Um, a little privacy, please*, or *This conversation is rated MA for Mature Audiences only*. They'd speak in whispers and lead their friends into rooms with doors that slammed shut. They'd beg Fonda to do their chores when they had their periods and forget to thank her. Their lack of regard hurt like a thousand ear-piercing guns to the heart. When Drew and Ruthie were around, it hurt a lot less, but even then, Fonda couldn't shake the desire to get her sisters' approval.

Luckily, Amelia was starting high school and Fonda would finally be the only Miller at Poplar Middle. Boys wouldn't ask her which beach her sisters would be at over the weekend, and girls wouldn't ask where they shopped. All questions directed at Fonda would be about Fonda. There would not be an older, cooler version of herself roaming the halls. For once, Fonda would be the Miller who mattered. Maybe she'd finally even earn the attention of the Avas, the only girls at Poplar Middle that Amelia had ever talked to. Fonda couldn't help but wonder what made three girls with identical names and personalities so special. They never once even *glanced* at Fonda, they were so busy laughing and tossing their effortless waves.

By nine thirty that night, everything Fonda wanted in seventh grade had been pasted into place. Yes, her feet ached and her paper cuts stung, but if manifesting goals really worked, Fonda would be so busy dominating she'd forget about her sisters forgetting about her.

For starters, she'd finally belong to a friend group. *Her* friend group. No more drifting from one squad to another or scrambling for a seat at lunch like she had to in sixth, after Maddie and Kaia, her closest elementary friends, transferred to private. From now on, Fonda's seat would be saved, and if she didn't show up, two people would notice. The Avas would no longer seem to have it all, because Fonda, Drew, and Ruthie would *actually* have it all. For the first time ever, they were going to the same school, and they'd show the Avas what true friendship looked like. So long, backstabbing, social climbing, and snobby side-eye glances. The nesties were going to set trends, spread joy, and support each other like underwire bras.

Fonda stepped back from the kitchen table to admire the fashion magazine clippings on her board. Goal number two was to become the leading voice in seventh-grade style. Yes, she'd have to do it wearing her sister's hand-me-downs, but she would be fearless about it. Mixing patterns with reckless abandon would be her thing. Take *that*, Winfrey's crop tops and Amelia's statement sunglasses. There's gonna be a new influencer in town!

"What does this symbolize?" Joan asked, pointing to the red circle in the top right corner.

"My body goals," Fonda said, her face turning the color of that circle.

"What body goals? Your body is perfect the way it is."

Fonda rolled her eyes. "You're just saying that because you're my mom."

"No," Joan said, "I'm saying it because it's true. You should be thanking your body every day for—"

"For what, being lazy?"

"No, for keeping you healthy."

"This isn't about *health*, Mom."

"Said no one sick, ever." Joan twisted her wild crimson curls into a bun and fastened them with a clean chopstick.

Fonda's flat chest tightened. Her mother was right, and she resented her for it. Or maybe she resented herself for being so shallow. But how was she supposed to be thankful for something that made her feel less important than her sisters? She never went mother-daughter bra shopping. She never got acne facials from that German woman named Katrine. And she certainly never got to eat snickerdoodles for dinner when she had period cramps.

"It's just that I'm thirteen, and I haven't—" Fonda lifted her gaze to the ceiling fan and blinked back her tears. Kids cried, not teens.

Joan bit down on her lip, fighting the urge to smile. "Honey, most kids your age are insecure and will try to make you feel as terrible as they do. Don't fall for it. Love yourself no matter what anyone says, and your body will develop when it's ready. In the meantime, appreciate who you are today because 'today' will never come back again."

"Wow," Fonda muttered. "That is seriously depressing."

With a warm grin, Joan cracked open a fortune cookie and handed Fonda the paper inside. It read *Your golden opportunity is coming shortly.*

Fonda took it from her mother and read it again. Then one more time.

If this fortune meant what she wanted it to mean, what she *needed* it to mean, Fonda was going to start a popular friend group with Drew and Ruthie, set the seventh-grade style trends, grow, blossom, and be treated like an equal by her sisters. If the fortune was right, this was going to be the best year of Fonda's life.

And if it was wrong?

Well, that simply wasn't an option.

chapter two.

DREW HARDEN'S FAVORITE place at Battleflag Family Camp was the infirmary. Specifically, during the hour that followed breakfast, and for reasons she preferred to keep to herself. But when someone asked why, which someone often did, she'd say, "The infirmary is the only cabin with a fan." And that shut them up pretty fast.

With another season coming to an end, Drew was there helping Nurse Cate pack up. Not so much for the reason she preferred to keep to herself but because Cate had been Drew's mentor over the summer. More "cool babysitter" than "medical professional," she taught Drew how to treat abrasions, sunburns, and bee stings so that she could follow her dream of becoming a nurse one day too.

Last semester, on Dream Job Day at St. Catherine's, the private girls' school Drew no longer had to attend, her leadership teacher expressed concern over Drew's "lack of ambition." *Nurse? Why not aim for doctor or surgeon?* she scribbled under the B-minus grade on Drew's essay. To which Drew thought, *Clearly this woman has never been to an emergency room.*

As a ride-or-die skateboarder, Drew had had her share of injuries, and the ER nurses always made her feel better. They also got to clean the blood and guts before the doctors arrived, and Drew was fascinated by blood and guts. Not in a serial-killer sort of way. Hers was more of a healthy curiosity, the kind parents encourage. *What does all that stuff in my body look like? Feel like? And how did twenty-five feet of intestines fit in there?* Sure, there were countless books and videos available to answer these questions, but nothing could replace a real-life glimpse at the goods. Like poorly wrapped birthday presents, wounds were opportunities to peek inside.

Had Drew been able to participate in the camp's activities, the infirmary might have been less appealing, but her parents owned Battleflag, which meant she and her older brother, Doug, weren't there to play; they were there to work. They got paid, so it wasn't like they were indentured servants or anything, but they couldn't exactly skate all day either. Drew got one day off a week to swim in the lake, ride the half-pipe, swing on the ropes course, and make friendship bracelets for Fonda and Ruthie, who she missed even more than fro-yo. But socializing with campers was off-limits.

"The guests are here to bond with *their* families, not ours," her parents often reminded her. But they didn't say anything about staying away from the infirmary after breakfast. So there she was, unplugging wires, packing up tongue depressors, and stealing glimpses of the microwave clock. Again, she had her reasons.

"Here he comes," Cate announced, with a sing-songy lilt.

Drew flushed with heat. "Here *who* comes?" she asked, knowing exactly who.

"Will Wilder. He shows up every morning after breakfast to take his allergy medicine, or haven't you noticed?"

"Haven't noticed."

Drew checked herself in the window's reflection.

Her blond ponytail was high and tight, her forehead was zit-free, and her peach tank made her tan skin look even tanner. And if Will had an issue with cutoff shorts and checkered Vans, well, Will would have to get over it. Because after six years of wearing kilts and blazers to private school, Drew was going public. She was finally allowed to choose her outfits, and she was choosing comfortable. So if Will preferred fancy eek-a-mouse types who wore miniskirts and sandals, Will was out of luck. Not that he'd have any way of knowing that, since they had never actually talked.

"There's a baggie in the fridge marked *Wilder*. Would you mind getting it for him?" Cate asked, then turned to her laptop and began typing, even though the power was off.

"Me?" Drew screeched. "Why me?"

Cate looked up and whispered, "Because camp is over. This is your last chance."

"Last chance for *what*?"

"To talk to him."

"What makes you think I want to talk to him?"

Cate raised her thick eyebrows. "Um, maybe because you're in here every morning."

"So?"

"So, I never need help in the morning, and you know it. You're here because this is when Will comes for his allergy medicine."

"It is?" Drew giggled, totally busted.

Cate closed her laptop. "Talk to him."

"I've been at an all-girls school for the last six years. I don't know how."

"Well, then you better figure it out," Cate said.

The hollow stomp of sneakers against the wood steps cut their conversation short. They also sent Cate running for a bathroom she didn't have to use.

"No! Don't go!"

"Back soon!"

The screen door squeaked open, and in loped Will.

Dressed in a grass-stained white tee and army-green shorts, he had the rumpled good looks of a Nickelodeon star after a long day on set. His messy blond hair seemed to be begging for a back-to-school cut, while the smirk behind his denim-blue eyes said, *Keep begging.* Here was a guy who cared more about winning the camp's iron-man challenges (he always did!) than perfecting his look. Which is exactly what made his look perfect. But mostly, Drew was drawn to the sides of Will she couldn't see but sensed. He seemed fun but not reckless. Kind but not boring. Competitive but not cutthroat. Basically, the male version of her.

Not that it mattered. Once she gave Will his medicine, they'd probably never see each other again.

"Hey," he said in that gravelly voice of his. "I'm here to pick up my—"

"Levocetirizine," Drew blurted. Then, faster than he could say *stalker*, she hurried for the fridge.

"The nurse has a Krown Rookie?" he asked, bending down to check out the skateboard propped next to the door.

Drew giggled. As if Nurse Cate would ever ride around camp on a pink board with purple flames. She was more of a natural-finish type. "It's mine," she called.

"I've seen you skate. You're good."

Drew returned with his baggie and a shy grin. "Thanks."

"I wanted to skate with you, but . . ."

"But what?" she asked, faking casual.

"I could *never* get away from my unit," he said, making fun of the Battleflag motto. *Family Units Unite!*

"Sticking with your family is what makes it a family," Drew added, quoting the camp song, which was actually quoting a famous author named Mitch . . . something.

"Yeah." Will rubbed the back of his neck. "All that togetherness can be pretty intense."

"Try growing up here," Drew said.

Will laughed a little.

Drew laughed a little back.

He glanced down at his red sneaks.

She glanced toward the bathroom. Where was Cate?

"Cool necklace," Drew said, desperate to fill the silence, but also drawn to the string of ivory shells, which reminded her of Maui's necklace from *Moana*.

His hand went straight to it, as if checking to make sure it was still there. "I made it during family arts and crafts."

"Cool."

The silence returned, only thicker this time. Packed with the embarrassment that comes from not knowing what to say next. At the same time, the chatter inside Drew's head was at full volume. *Talk.*

Be clever and charming. Not too charming, or he'll think you're flirting. Not too clever, or he'll think you're showing off. Hurry! If you don't, he'll leave. Wait, maybe it's better if he leaves. I mean, he's going to leave at some point, so why not get it over with? Ugh! If I hadn't spent the last six years at a private girls' school, I'd know what to say. Fonda would know what to say. Her sisters would definitely know what to say. Ruthie might or might not know what to say, but if she didn't, she'd lay one of her "fun facts" on him, and it would seem like she knew. I wish they were here right now. I have to remember what Will looks like so I can describe him to them. Oh no, we just made eye contact. Look away!

"How'd you get that scar?" Will asked, indicating the thin white line between Drew's upper lip and left nostril.

"Zombie." She blushed. The scar was so faint. If Will had noticed it, it meant he wasn't just looking at her; he was *looking* at her.

"Blindfold tag?"

Drew nodded. *No one ever knew what Zombie was!* "It happened when I was nine. Face, meet tree branch. Tree branch, meet face."

Will nodded like he knew that story all too well. "Have you ever played Zombie on your skateboard?"

"No. You?"

"The parking lot at my school was paved last year. So we play on weekends."

"Sounds like a fun school."

"Yeah," Will said. "On weekends."

Drew laughed a little.

Will laughed a little back.

"Where do you go to school?"

"Poplar Middle."

Drew cocked her head, sure she hadn't heard him properly. "Wait, where?"

"Poplar Middle."

"Shut up!" Drew said, smacking him on the arm. "Really?"

"Uh, yeah." Will rubbed his arm. "You know it?"

"That's where I'm going!"

"Seriously?" Will's cheeks reddened. "Seventh?"

"Yep."

"How have I never seen you there before?"

"I was at St. Catherine's. I'm starting Poplar this year. Are the teachers strict?"

"Don't get me stah-ted," Will said; then he turned even redder. "Sorry. It's a line from this old skateboard movie I found on YouTube. It's super cheesy, but I'm kind of obsessed."

"*The Skateboard Kid*?"

"You *know* it?"

Drew smiled a smile that felt too wide for her face. "My brother, Doug, and I watch it all the time."

"No way."

"Way!"

The screen door screeched open, then stuttered shut behind a fit brunette woman wearing a wide-brimmed hat, a Battleflag tank top, and a toxic amount of insect repellant.

"There you are, Will," she said, offering Drew a polite grin. "Did you get your medicine? Your father and sister are waiting in the car."

Drew handed Will the bag.

"Thanks," Will said, more to the bag than Drew. "So I guess I'll see you at school."

"Not if you're playing Zombie."

"Huh?"

"You'll be blindfolded."

"True." Will ran a hand through his hair. Blond peaks formed in its wake. It looked like a dinosaur's spine. "Anyway, you should play with us sometime."

"Sounds good," Drew said, anxious to know when, exactly, so she could hurry up and get there.

"Will, let's go!" said his mother.

"I better—"

"Yeah."

"Okay."

"Bye," Drew said, with a stiff wave. The kind that says, *My hand is on board for this goodbye, but my heart is not.* Drew blinked, taking a mental video of its floppy, this-hurts-me-more-than-it-hurts-you quality, then filed it under To Be Analyzed by Ruthie and Fonda. She'd be back with her nesties in no time and couldn't wait to tell them every single detail. Twice.

chapter three.

THE WHITE HOUSE was majestic. The Capitol reflecting pool at dusk had been magical. And all seventeen United States memorials had moved the Goldman family to tears. But the reunion that was about to take place in Ruthie's bedroom would be the most memorable part of her summer, by far.

No offense, Washington, DC, she thought as she emptied the errant almond shards, pencil shavings, and six crossword puzzle books from her travel backpack. Ruthie enjoyed the adventure with her parents—it was an all-you-can-eat buffet for her brain. But her brain was full. She was ready to be home. Home is where the heart is, after all, and her heart had been left behind to starve. The fact that she was not allowed to use electronic devices, not even to stay in touch with friends, made that hunger even worse. She'd hoped for a squealing driveway reunion, but Fonda was grocery shopping with her sisters and Drew had only gotten back from camp thirty minutes ago and was also unpacking.

But none of that mattered, because they were going to arrive at her house in—Ruthie consulted her pink Timex—five minutes! That was three hundred seconds until their Friday-night sleepover, the first one in two months, began.

Ruthie couldn't wait to hear Drew's hilarious descriptions of the Battleflag campers and how Fonda managed to work three jobs. She couldn't wait to pick chips off their plates without having to ask permission, laugh at their burps, and eventually fall asleep to the sound of their collective breathing. She couldn't wait to be back with her girls, once and for all.

With that, Ruthie scooped up Foxie, the last item on her rug, and tucked her into bed. Foxie was her secret, beloved stuffie that only her besties and her parents knew she still had. Ruthie first spotted it five years earlier, in the second-grade lost-and-found.

Foxie's pointy snout had poked out from the jumble of sweatshirts, sneakers, and lunch boxes like a snorkel. The poor thing was all alone. Ruthie had no choice but to rescue her, especially with the oodles they had in common:

1. Dark eyes alight with curiosity
2. Perky ears, alert and ready to learn
3. Sibling-free
4. Lonely
5. Fondness for the word *oodles*

Ruthie's doorbell rang, followed by the usual round of Morse code knocks: one long sound followed by two quick ones for the letter *D*. Then two short, one long, one short, for *F*. Her pack was back! Moments later, she, Drew, and Fonda were fused together in a three-way hug, bouncing around her bedroom and squealing with joy. The eight-week friend fast was officially over.

"Your hair!" Ruthie said to Fonda. What had once been cinnamon brown and curly was now sleek, shiny, and past her collarbone.

"I bought a flat iron with my babysitting money," Fonda said, stroking the ends. "You like?"

"I do!" Ruthie enthused. But if she were being totally honest, she would have said she missed the curls. They were friendly, approachable, and up for anything. Without them, Fonda appeared older, more serious. Like someone who had a long to-do list and was determined to get it done.

Next, she complimented Drew's hair, which looked extra blond from the summer sun.

"And *you* look . . ." Drew searched Ruthie's pale, summer-is-for-reading skin.

"The exact same," Fonda said, completing the sentence.

They were right. Ruthie was still taller than Fonda and shorter than Drew. Her wide blue eyes remained mascara free. Her two-inch bangs and chin-length bob hadn't changed a bit. (How anyone could see the French film *Amélie* and not copy Audrey Tautou's haircut was a wig scratcher.)

"Same is good," Ruthie said, pleased. Predictability made her feel safe. Then, "Wait, I *do* have something new!" She pointed at the wall behind her bed. Like the other walls in her room, it was decorated with puzzles she had completed over the years, but this particular wall had a new addition. "Can you spot it?"

Drew and Fonda jumped up on the mattress to get a closer look.

"You moved the sandy beach next to the black cats?" Drew guessed.

"The beach has always been by the cats," Fonda said. "Is the snowstorm new?"

"She's had that since fourth grade," Drew said.

"True . . ." Fonda said, tap-tapping her chin.

Ruthie's concern morphed into excitement. There was nothing more exhilarating than a memory challenge. "Give up?"

"NO!" they both said.

Then, after a few seconds, Drew shouted, "The Washington Monument!"

"Correct!"

"I win!" Drew did a victory dance on the bed. Not because she wanted to gloat, but because competition was in her DNA. The Hardens literally ate cereal out of first-place-trophy cups.

"Snack attack!" Fonda said as she cleared the

cushions from Ruthie's reading nook and presented her offerings to the group: brownies, Red Vines, Sun Chips, and the requisite oranges. As always, she hid everything under a blanket except the oranges, which she placed on Ruthie's desk in case her mom came in.

Dr. Fran Goldman, a pediatrician, was dead set against processed foods, and insisted that all snacks be made in her kitchen, using only natural ingredients. The pantry was basically floor-to-ceiling heart-healthy almonds and raisins. And honestly, only toddlers and grandparents liked raisins. The situation at Drew's was equally tragic, since her parents were always on some kind of high-protein caveman diet. Fonda's pantry, however, was a wonderland. Joan was so determined to raise independent women she had her daughters do the grocery shopping. The only rule was, if you got a cavity, you paid for the filling. So, after every indulgence, Fonda would floss right there, mid-sleepover. Was it gross? Yes. Did they care? Of course not.

The next hour was a blur of sugary snacks and catch-up: Ruthie wanted the play-by-play of each and every day she'd been kept apart from her friends, and they were happy to fill her in on every detail. Finally satisfied she knew it all, she flopped back against a pillow.

"Three more sleeps until Poplar Middle," Ruthie announced, thrilled that for the first time ever, they would all be at the same school. Same schedules, same teachers, same friends. Her old school was anti-cliques, anti-grades, anti-technology, anti–birthday parties, anti-plastic, anti-sugar, and anti-fun. There was only one good thing about Forest Day: it stopped after sixth grade. "I can't wait to sit together in every class." Ruthie was picturing them like puzzle pieces, snapping together with zero effort, three perfect fits.

Fonda popped open the bag of Sun Chips. "I can't wait to have lunch together."

"And walk to school together," Drew added.

"And pee together."

"And study together."

"And see each other in the halls."

"And go to the same parties."

"And dances."

"And field trips."

"And Will," Drew blurted.

"*Will?*" Ruthie asked, wondering if she'd heard wrong. "We make wills in middle school?"

"No." Drew bit into a Red Vine. "Will Wilder."

"How do you know Will?" Fonda asked with a mouth full of chips.

"So . . . there's one little thing I forgot to tell you," Drew said. Her cheeks were red as she replayed her infirmary conversation with Will in such detail Ruthie could almost smell the rubber soles of his red sneakers, see his shell necklace, taste his allergy medicine. The more Drew said, the brighter her T-zone glistened not from zit-producing oils, but from over-stimulated crush glands.

The only right way to feel in that moment was happy for Drew. So why did Ruthie want to grab Foxie, sniff the part of her ear that smelled like bananas, and cry? Why did the idea of Drew snapping into place with a new puzzle piece fill Ruthie with panic? It wasn't like Drew said she was *unsnapping* with Ruthie. In fact, Drew didn't say *anything* about Ruthie, just Will. Maybe that was the problem. After eight weeks apart, why wasn't Drew talking about missing her and Fonda? She'd told them everything about family camp, but she hadn't actually said she *missed* them.

"This will be good for my goal." Fonda's brown eyes looked golden as the setting sun came through the window.

"I knew it!" Ruthie said, relieved Fonda was taking control, as always. "That hair is all business."

"You have a Will goal?" Drew asked, confused.

"Yeah," Fonda said. "As in we *will* dominate."

Drew handed Ruthie the Red Vines; Ruthie handed Drew a brownie. They were all ears.

"What do you want to dominate?" Ruthie dared to ask.

"Seventh grade."

Ruthie and Drew exchanged a quick glance. They knew Fonda envied her older sisters. How they never needed Google to know what to wear or say or do. They just knew, without searching a single thing. They never doubted their decisions or questioned their outfits. They never walked away from conversations wondering if they sounded silly. Her besties also knew Fonda was tired of living in their perfume-scented shadows. That she wanted to step into the spotlight and be seen. But dominate? Only cartoon villains wanted that.

"How are you going to do it?" Drew asked.

"Not me," Fonda said. "*We*."

Ruthie bit down on her thumbnail. Her goals for Poplar Middle were a little more basic:

1. Have fun with her best friends
2. Maintain a 100 percent average
3. Don't get lost

"Domination seems a little lofty for us newbies, don't you think?" Ruthie looked to Drew. "Maybe we should shoot for something more realistic, like 'Make a new friend by Halloween'—"

Fonda crumpled up the empty bag of Sun Chips. "There's no time for *realistic*. The Avas are already posting about some boy-girl party they're throwing in October, and school hasn't even started yet. But if Will is in the mix, maybe we can throw our own boy-girl party."

"What's with you and the Avas?" Ruthie asked, wondering why three girls with the same name were so important to Fonda, why she brought them up in conversation at least once a week. She never referenced the funny things they said, their mind-expanding hobbies, or the contributions, if any, they were making to society. All she talked about was how great they thought they were and that they never let anyone sit with them at lunch. "You've been obsessing over them for years. I don't get it."

"I'm only obsessed with them because everyone else is obsessed with them, and they don't deserve all that attention. We do." Fonda palmed her straight hair. "Now that we're going to be together, we can start our own thing. You know, show the Avas how fun is done."

"I have an idea!" Drew said. She retrieved her Battleflag overnight bag and pulled a Ziploc baggie from the outside pocket. Inside were three pink-and-gray beaded bracelets with the letters *FDR* in the center.

"Best US president ever," Ruthie gushed.

"More like our initials, nerd," Drew teased. "They're our new friendship bracelets." The girls held out their arms while Drew fastened her latest creations to their wrists. They now had eight matching bracelets in total.

"It's a great start," Fonda said. "But we need something else."

"A necklace?" Ruthie suggested.

"No, a strategy. And I have one. It's called LIKES."

"As in Will likes Zombie, and so do I?" Drew said.

In an effort to be supportive, Ruthie laughed. Normally Fonda would have laughed too, but that all-business hair of hers wasn't having it.

"Each letter stands for a different part of the plan," she explained. "So, *L* is for *lunch*. If we sit in the same seats at the same table every day, people will see us as an established group. *I* is for *inseparable*. We stay together as much as possible."

Ruthie let out a happy squeak. She was so over being apart.

"*K* is for *kind*," Fonda continued. "The nicer we are, the more people will want to hang out with us. And the goal is to make everyone want to hang out with us. So, think eye contact and smiles."

Drew and Ruthie nodded.

"*E* is for *extra* because everything we do has to be extra awesome. And *S* is for *style*." She flicked a glance at Ruthie's pineapple print romper and Drew's plaid pajama bottoms, which she sometimes wore to the movies. "I say we pick a color of the day, every day, and we all have to wear it. I plan on mixing a lot of patterns this season, so think more dominant color than monochromatic, but I'm open to suggestions."

Drew's hand shot up. "Can the boys wear our dominant colors too, or is this strictly a girl thing?"

"Thirsty much?" Fonda teased.

"Yes," Drew said. "Very much. And you would be too if you spent the last six years at an all-girls school."

"What exactly are you thirsty for?" Ruthie pressed. She wasn't ready for crushes and kisses. And she wasn't ready for Drew to be ready either.

"Nothing." Drew twisted the end of her ponytail. "Just someone to skate with." Her cheeks grew red. "Can we move on now, please?"

They spent the rest of the night swapping stories about their summers and debating which color they should wear on the first day of school. Fonda wanted red because it was strong. Drew wanted purple because it matched the flames on her skateboard. And Ruthie wanted plaid because it included all the colors. But they agreed on one thing: seventh grade was going to be a game changer, and Fonda was playing to win.

chapter four.

THE FIRST DAY of school was postcard perfect. Sunlight saturated the cul-de-sac and illuminated the flowers like crown jewels. It was the kind of morning that smacked of Instagram filters and laundry detergent commercials: the hues and tones were *that* bright. But much to Fonda's disappointment, the color love stopped there.

"We agreed on the COD last night," she told Drew and Ruthie on their inaugural walk to Poplar Middle. "And the Color of the Day was red." Fonda could hear the frustration in her voice, feel its weight crush her bones. Because, come on. Red symbolized passion and fire. It transformed lips with a single swipe and literally stopped traffic. Why were they fighting that?

"That's exactly why I wore *this*." Drew pointed at the

diamond-shaped logo on her green tee. Yes, it was red. It was also the size of a grape. Fonda understood that after years of wearing a uniform, Drew wanted to be comfortable. But green? It didn't make people stop. It told them to keep going. And Ruthie's romper was no better.

"The cherries are red," Ruthie argued.

Fonda wanted to scream, but she stopped herself. They had ten months to get this COD thing right. The important thing was that they were finally together.

A horde of students had gathered at the school crosswalk and were waiting for the light to change. Normally, Fonda would have slowed down to avoid the awkwardness of standing with them. Today, however, she sped up. Her plan was to be visible when she told Drew and Ruthie about her revolutionary new accessory, because whispers and giggles would definitely follow, and nothing said *we're the fun group* like three girls wearing matching friendship bracelets and whisper-giggling at eight fifteen in the morning.

"Check this out," Fonda said, pulling a white canvas bag with red polka dots from her backpack. Her voice was louder than it needed to be, considering she, Drew, and Ruthie were practically touching. But Fonda wanted to pique the interest of the other kids, and with the passing cars and app sounds wafting off nearby phones, vocal projection was the only way to command attention.

"Cute pencil case!" Drew gushed.

"It's not a pencil case," Fonda said. "It's a"—she gestured for them to lean closer—"period purse."

Ruthie drew back her head. "What's a—"

Fonda slapped a hand over Ruthie's mouth. "Shhh," she said with an exaggerated laugh and a casual side-eye glance at her audience. And yes, they were side-eyeing her back. Mission accomplished!

Omitting the part about getting the idea from her sisters, Fonda quietly explained that it was stocked with menstrual essentials so she'd never get caught off guard.

Drew gasped. "Hold up! When did you get your . . . P? Why didn't you tell us?"

"I didn't," Fonda said. "But when I do, I'll be prepared."

"Why does your period need a purse?"

"It's going to be very fahn-cy," Ruthie said with a terrible British accent.

They giggled. Heads turned. It was perfect.

A peppy woman wearing an orange vest stepped into the crosswalk and waved the students forward. Fonda's audience dissipated, but her plan had worked. Next time any one of those kids saw her, they'd think, *There's that girl from the crosswalk. The one who had friendship bracelets and secrets on the first day.*

"I still don't get why you need that," Ruthie said as they approached the busy campus.

"A woman's first period can come at any time. When it does, she'll need pads, a change of underwear, essential oils to help with cramps, and Reese's Pieces."

"Why RPs?"

"They're delicious."

"I want a period purse," Ruthie said.

Fonda beamed. "I'll get right on it."

"Hashtag me too," added Drew.

"That's such an inappropriate use of hashtag me too," Ruthie explained.

"Hashtag not now," Fonda sighed as the bustling Great Lawn of Poplar Middle came into view. "It's showtime." With that, she rolled back her shoulders, jutted her chin, and cat-walked toward the chaos like Victoria's best-kept secret. Yes, her red-striped tank dress and leopard-print high-tops were on point, but this sudden burst of confidence was about more than fashion, even more than friends. It was about hope. The kind associated with fresh starts and second chances.

With a shaky hand, Fonda slid off one of the straps from her backpack (only elementary kids slung over both) and linked arms with Drew and Ruthie. The COD disaster was behind them. They were back on track.

"Wow." Ruthie stopped, taking it all in. "This is just like the movies . . ." She shielded her eyes from the glaring sun to marvel at the line of SUVs inching toward the drop-off area, the reuniting friends, the introverts slouching over smartphones, and the American flag at the center of it all. "This is nothing like Forest Day. It's"—she pulled Fonda and Drew closer—"a lot."

"It's not so bad," Fonda said, surprising herself. In the past, she thought of the two glass wings that extended off the main entrance as open blades on a Swiss Army knife. Steely and cold. Now they were outstretched arms, there to welcome her into the mix. A mix that no longer included Winfrey or Amelia. A mix made entirely of her own ingredients—including her two best friends.

Drew shook her head. "I can't believe I can wear shorts to school."

Fonda beamed, as if the relaxed dress code had been her idea. "You guys are gonna love it here."

"No more skirts!" Drew dropped her backpack to the grass and did a cartwheel, right there in front of everyone. "I'm freeeee!"

Fonda flushed. She wanted attention, but was this the kind of attention she wanted? *Yes. Yes it is,* she thought upon noticing that a few kids were watching. Even the three Avas glanced over as they passed by. Fonda smiled. Drew was just being herself, as always. It occurred to Fonda that was actually pretty cool.

"That was extra," Ruthie said as Drew picked up her backpack.

"Yep." Fonda smiled. "She just put the *E* in LIKES."

"I'd rather put the *he* in *schedule,*" Drew said, cheeks flushed, ponytail askew.

Ruthie and Fonda looked back at her, confused.

"*Will,*" Drew said. "I want to know if he's in any of my classes."

"Come," Fonda said, as if Drew's comment didn't make her feel the tiniest bit hurt. She was happy to fold

Will into the mix, but not today. Today was supposed to be about *them.* "Let's find out," she managed to say anyway.

With pride, Fonda led the girls down the crowded glass hallway toward the gym. "The ceilings are retractable. They stay open when the weather is nice."

"So . . . always?" Ruthie said, squinting up at the sentinel of palm trees standing watch overhead.

"Yep, pretty much."

Confidence strengthened Fonda's voice and fueled her strides as she indicated where the bathrooms were, named the boring teachers, and pointed out the vending machine that gave back extra change.

Once in the gym, the girls splintered off to get their schedules, each one heading to the table marked with the first letter of her last name. While Fonda waited with the other Ms, she greeted the familiar faces with a warm smile and a wave. Each time someone waved back, joy ricocheted through her entire body. She had this.

"Yes!" she said to Drew once they reconvened on the bleachers. "We have four out of six classes together. Everything but PE and math." She searched the crowd, wondering what was taking Ruthie so long.

Then Ruthie appeared, waving her schedule as she approached. "I don't get it. How am I supposed to know where my classes are?"

"The room number is printed on your schedule," Fonda said, "next to the subject."

"Not mine."

"Let me see that." Fonda swiped the paper from Ruthie's hand. As she scanned the columns, those ricocheting jolts of joy morphed into stabs of pain. "Oh no . . ."

Ruthie sat. "What?"

"This is bad."

Ruthie stood. *"What?"*

"Is she in trouble?" Drew asked.

"Worse."

"What?" Drew and Ruthie said at the same time.

"You're in TAG."

"Meaning?"

"The Talented and Gifted program. It's a whole other thing. Totally. Separate. From us."

Ruthie's mouth froze in the shape of an O. Her blue eyes glistened with tears. "But we were supposed to be *together*."

"I know," Fonda said, her once-strong voice now barely audible. Her seventh-grade vision was ruined. They were not going to be inseparable. They were not going to share jokes about teachers. They would not be invited to the same birthday parties.

"Can we change it?" Drew tried.

"Maybe," Fonda said, even though she was pretty sure class assignments were definite. "We can still have lunch together."

"And walk home together," Drew added.

Ruthie sniffled. "Can we pee together?"

Fonda looked down at her high-tops. "I'm pretty sure you have your own bathrooms."

The five-minute bell sounded. Everyone headed for the doors, everyone except them. While rubbing soothing circles on Ruthie's slumped back, Fonda couldn't help wondering if her vision board needed glasses, because this was the opposite of what she was trying to manifest. Not that it mattered. The damage was done.

"We better go," Fonda sighed. "Tardy is no way to stardy."

"We'll meet you after school." Drew pouted as they parted ways in the hall.

"Bye," Ruthie mouthed, as if her throat were too dry to speak. Then she slow-waved and shuffled off in the opposite direction.

"There goes the *I* in LIKES," Fonda said, because, as of that moment, *inseparable* was in-possible.

chapter five.

THE TAG PROGRAM was small: four boys, five girls, and one teacher who wore a shapeless orange dress, gray flats, and a curious black bob she continuously forced behind her ears. Their classroom didn't look like anything Ruthie was used to. The desks were round tables, there were balance balls instead of chairs, and glass doors opened onto a private garden.

"Welcome back, Titans!" said the teacher. Her name, *Rhea Alden (but call me Rhea)*, was written on the whiteboard behind her, the sight of which made Ruthie smile out loud. If only Drew and Fonda were there, they would be cracking up. Instead, she had to pretend a woman named after loose stool was perfectly normal. "I hope you had an enriching summer! Come in—take a seat!"

Ruthie tried to sit, but the giant ball under her butt put up a fight. She had to grip her desk to stabilize.

"It helps if you suck in your abs," whispered the skinny boy to her right. The name on his folder read *Everest Bolden.*

"Good morning, Titans!" Rhea said.

Titans? Did the teacher really just refer to them as Titans?

Ruthie had never felt so imbalanced in her life. How was she going to survive in this alternate universe? A place where students were referred to as Titans and the simple act of sitting required extreme core engagement?

"We have a great new mind among us today. Welcome, Ruthie! We are going to have fun learning together. As the founding father of genetics, Gregor Mendel, says, Whoo-pea!"

The class tittered, and Ruthie cracked a smile— Gregor Mendel did his experiments with pea plants. It was the kind of corny science joke Ruthie loved, that no one else ever got.

"Titans, like the deities in Greek mythology, you are powerful, and influential . . ."

Ruthie peeled her hands off her desk and tried to balance. She swayed left and grabbed back on while glimpsing the clock above the bookshelves. Three more hours until lunch with Drew and Fonda.

"Everyone *thinks* TAG stands for Talented and Gifted," Rhea continued. "But I *know* it means Titans Are . . ."

Eight hands shot up while Ruthie's remained down, fixed to the edge of her desk to avoid tipping over.

"Every day after the pledge, we come up with a new word for the *G* in TAG," Rhea informed Ruthie. Then she pointed at the redhead in the denim jumpsuit beside Everest. "Yes, Alberta?"

"Titans Are Giants," she said.

"Quite literally," Rhea said, pleased. "Titans were giants who ruled the heavens, and that's what I expect from all of you this year. I want you to rule the—"

Ruthie raised her hand, lost her balance, and slid onto the floor.

Rhea's eyes flashed compassion. "They take a bit of getting used to, but once you do, you'll be amazed at how charged your mind will feel. Something to add, Ruthie?"

Ruthie's heart began to pound, a Morse code message to cease and desist. "It's okay. I'm good. It was just a random fun fact."

"No, really—share." Rhea smiled. "We worship fun facts, don't we, Titans?"

No one nodded.

"See?" Rhea said, oblivious. "Go on, tell us."

"I was going to say that technically, after the ten-year war, the Titans were overthrown by the Olympians, then imprisoned in the Underworld for all of eternity. So yes, they ruled heaven, but not for very long."

Rhea hooked her hair behind her ear. "True, but unfortunately, we can't call ourselves Olympians."

"Why not?"

"There's no O in TAG."

The students laughed.

"What if we named ourselves Troubadours or Tigers or . . . Oh, Trailblazers would be fun!"

A girl let out a giggle, then quickly looked down. A curtain of straight pink hair covered her mouth, and her eyes were obscured by thick black frames. Was she giggling *with* Ruthie or *at* her?

"Thank you for your input, Ruthie. I admire your

pluck," Rhea said. "But I just placed an order for Titans spirit wear, so let's do our best to focus on their good years, okay?"

"Okay," Ruthie said, even though it wasn't. Nothing about misrepresenting Greek mythology was okay.

"Now that that's settled, can I have a volunteer to show Ruthie around?"

The pink-haired girl raised her hand.

"Great, thank you, Sage. All remaining Titans, please grab your baskets and join me in the garden."

"There's some serious BTE in this room, am I right?" Sage asked, once everyone had gone.

"What's BTE?"

"Big Titan Energy. Come, I'll give you a tour."

Outside the oversized windows, the rest of the class was settling in a circle beneath a Japanese maple tree.

Sage started with a cabinet at the back of the room, which was divided into six sections. "Each one contains the materials we use for our seated subjects. Go ahead," Sage said, proud. "Take a look."

Ruthie lifted one section and found the books they'd be reading for literature. She lifted another and saw a sophisticated geometry set. Inside the third was a microscope, protective goggles, tools, a laptop, and a brand-new iPhone. Ruthie quickly closed it back up.

"What's wrong?" Sage asked.

"I'm not allowed to use devices. My mom is worried about—"

"Your attention span?"

"No."

"Vision?"

"No."

"Online predators?"

"No. Radio frequency waves."

"Don't worry." Sage swiped her hand dismissively. "We don't *use* the devices. We take them apart. You know, to see how they work."

A glitter bomb exploded inside Ruthie's belly. Even though she missed Fonda and Ruthie, the TAG program was hard to hate. The classroom was spacious and modern; their outdoor space was a Zen den of tranquility. They even had a state-of-the-art kitchen for food science.

"Why don't the other kids get all this?" Ruthie asked, thinking of Drew and Fonda.

Sage peered over the top of her glasses. "Seriously?"

Ruthie nodded.

"In their world, *LOL* stands for laugh out loud. In ours, it's love of learning."

Ruthie frowned. That sounded so elitist. "But—"

"Look, is TAG different from the regular curriculum? Yes. Do the Titans have an incredible learning facility? Yes. But no one is giving it to us. We have four fund-raisers every year to pay for all of this. We work for it. You'll see."

"Impressive," Ruthie said. "But it doesn't change the fact that our teacher was named after a loose stool."

"It's pronounced Ray-a," Sage said flatly. "As in ray-a sun. Which she is. Trust me, you'll love her."

"Noted," Ruthie said, disappointed. She liked pronouncing it her way much better. "What time is lunch?"

"Depends."

"On what?"

"If we have a guest speaker, which we almost always do, in which case we eat outside in the pagoda and LTL."

Ruthie rolled her eyes, tired of asking what everything meant.

"Learn through lunch," Sage offered.

Ruthie longed for the comforting banana smell of Foxie's ear. "So, we don't eat lunch with everyone else?"

"Fear not, young Titan." Sage threw an arm around Ruthie's shoulder and squeezed. "You have us now."

In that moment, Ruthie really did feel like a Titan: cast into the underworld and doomed for all of eternity.

chapter six.

DREW SLAPPED HER lunch box down on a four-seater table. "What about this one?" she asked Fonda. "The extra chair can be for Will, who will probably swing by for dessert."

Unlike the scene at St. Catherine's, where students ate in a crowded, hot-dog-scented banquet room, meals at Poplar Middle were enjoyed outdoors, on green metal tables that, like a restaurant, came in different sizes.

Fonda peered out over the top of yellow sunglasses and evaluated. Her mission to find the perfect table, the perfect *everything*, surprised Drew. When they went to the movies, Fonda always let Drew and

Ruthie pick the seats. When the booths were taken at their favorite fro-yo shop, she'd shrug and pop a squat on the floor. Why did it suddenly matter where their table was? They were together! Their mission was already accomplished.

"I give it five stars," Drew tried. "No bird poop, centrally located, and right next to—" She hitched her thumb toward the boys beside them.

"Ew, no, they're *sixth* graders! Keep looking."

"For *what*?"

"Something close to the Avas, but not right next to them. Near the grass, but not on it. Under the canopy, but only half shaded."

Fonda eventually settled on a different four-top, one table away from the basketball courts and two down from the Avas' Fjällräven Kånken backpacks, which they must have laid down before lunch even started. The only thing missing now was Will, who wasn't in any of Drew's morning classes or the hallways in between. And, of course, Ruthie.

"Do you think she got lost?" Drew asked, peering back at the glass wings.

"The girl can do a five-hundred-piece puzzle in fifteen minutes, but she can't find the Lunch Garden. How is that even possible?"

Drew giggled. *Lunch Garden.* They really called it that.

"Dr. Fran needs to get her a phone already," Fonda said as she pressed her glossy lips against a skinny can of grapefruit Perrier and downed it in one gulp.

Baaaap.

Fonda covered her mouth and giggled.

"Excuse *you.*" Drew laughed, grateful for the burp. It proved that Fonda was still Fonda, even though she was trying really hard to be something else.

Two brunettes in matching denim skirts approached their table.

"Taken," Fonda said.

"You can't save," said the freckly one as she set down her tray.

"I'm not saving."

"Then why are there two empty seats here?"

"Our friend is in the restroom."

"There's room for one of you, though," Drew

offered, knowing that they'd never split up. Girls in matching outfits rarely did.

They exchanged a horrified look.

"Don't worry. We get it." Fonda grinned as she handed Freckles her tray. "I did see some open seats by the trash cans . . ."

"*You're* a trash can," said Freckles's friend as they left.

"That girl is no boomerang," Drew said once they were alone. "She's terrible at comebacks." Then she popped the top off her Tupperware. "Chicken dinos. Yes!"

Fonda stood. "Guard this table with your life."

"Where are you going?"

"To find Ruthie before someone else tries to steal her spot."

"Wait!" Drew bristled. "You can't just leave me here."

"I'll be right back," Fonda said. "Don't. Get. Up."

Drew bit into a cold dino. "Hurry."

Now alone, she became hyperaware of her surroundings. The swells of laughter, the crinkle of chip bags, the pop-hiss of soda cans being opened. She felt obvious, conspicuous, and impossible to miss: a gawky palm tree in a Lunch Garden of delicate flowers.

She wanted to study the boys. She wanted to know if any of the girls were into skating. She wanted to know if she'd always feel like an outsider. But more than anything, she wanted to know if Will was nearby.

The honeysuckle-scented breeze tickled the back of Drew's neck. Was he behind her . . . looking at her *right now*? Gazing at her ponytail with those denim-blue eyes of his? It was a level-five creepy thought that made her legs twitch. Then itch.

She wanted to scratch.

She wanted to turn.

She couldn't turn.

Turning would seem desperate. Instead, Drew examined her cuticles, trying to appear aloof. But ten cuticles only bought her ten seconds. After that, temptation crossed the finish line and won. Its prize: a full 360-degree perimeter scan. Which wasn't much of a prize, considering Will wasn't watching her at all. No one was.

Then came the familiar grind of polyurethane wheels on asphalt. Had her eye finally spied the guy?

Drew tracked the sound to the basketball courts. A force she could only describe as supernatural lifted her from her seat and guided her toward the blacktop, where she had the pleasure of watching Will stick a kickflip while his friend shot video. Her knees buckled a little. It was as if all twenty-five feet of Drew's intestines were being squashed by intense feelings. No wonder they called it a crush.

Next Will tic-tacked around his friend, and his relaxed stance made it look much easier than it was. Drew was daring herself to say hey when his wheels rolled over an empty Ziploc bag and the board slipped out from under him. He was on the ground now, spine curved like a croissant.

Drew's heart began to rev. Was Will hurt?

Fighting the urge to run, Drew moved calmly toward him because, according to Nurse Cate, running often caused victims to panic. And it was crucial for first responders to appear in control. But before she got close, Will popped back up and mounted his board, and the tic-tacking quickly resumed.

Now too close to watch from afar, Drew was forced to make contact. "Hey," she said, waving.

It was the moment in the story when Will was supposed to hop off his board, jog over, and greet her with an easy smile. But apparently this wasn't *that* movie. This was a reality show. One where Will saw Drew and then, with barely a nod in her direction, rode off in the opposite direction.

"There you are!" Fonda said, coming in hot. Her strides were determined, and her flat-ironed hair was pumping around her face like fish gills. "I went to our table, and you weren't there. You know who was, though? That freckly girl and three of her friends."

The table! "Oh no, I'm so sorry. I totally for—"

"It was the perfect spot! Now we have nothing."

"I—"

"Why did you get up?"

Drew pointed at the boys at the far end of the court, who were now playfully knocking into each other's boards. "Will," she squeaked.

"Oh," Fonda said, the furrow between her brows softening. "Did you talk to him?"

"No," Drew muttered. "He acted like he didn't know me."

"Maybe he has bad eyesight," Fonda tried.

"I hope so." Then, "Did you find Ruthie?"

"Sure did," Fonda said, gazing out at the distant peaks of the Santa Ana Mountains, as if remembering simpler times. "She's in her classroom."

"Doing what?"

"Learning through lunch."

"That's a thing?" It sounded even more stuck-up than Lunch Garden.

"Apparently."

"So she'll sit with us tomorrow?"

Fonda shook her head. "It's every day."

"For the entire year?"

"Yep."

A sleeping bag of sadness enveloped Drew. The only thing that got her through six years at St. Catherine's— where fitting in meant pretending to care about gossip, cupcake competition shows, and soccer—was knowing that, come seventh grade, she could go to school with Fonda and Ruthie. She could love skateboarding, hate hairbrushes, and choose to be a nurse instead of a doctor, without judgment. When the three of them were together, she could finally just be. But the three of them *weren't* together, and it felt as if Christmas had been canceled.

Drew and Fonda stood at the edge of the blacktop, silent and uneasy, trapped in the thick stickiness of not knowing what to do next.

"I'm sorry I left the table," Drew said, meaning it. Not only did she break her promise, she did it for a guy who didn't care enough to wave. "It wasn't even worth it."

The warmth returned to Fonda's eyes, and she grabbed Drew by the wrist. "Then let's make it worth it. Let's go talk to him."

"I can't."

"If you don't, we'll have lost our table for nothing, and I can't live with that."

"Fine," Drew sighed, grateful for Fonda's support but also a little bit nervous. What if he ignored her a second time?

With Fonda by her side, Drew moved toward Will with bouncy, friendly steps. "Hey," she called again.

The corners of his mouth lifted into a smile that quickly fell when his buddy rolled up.

"Hey," said the friend. "I'm Henry." Dark-eyed and deeply tanned, he had shaggy brown hair and the latest iPhone, which had only come out a day earlier.

"Yeah," Drew said, "I know who you are. You threw a ball at me in PE this morning."

"No fair," Fonda said. "You got to play dodgeball?"

"No. We ran track, which is why the whole ball thing was weird."

Henry's cheeks reddened. "Yeah, sorry about that."

"And you two already know each other, right?" Fonda said to Will.

Drew flashed her friend a grateful smile.

"You know her?" Henry asked Will, surprised. "How?"

Will ran a hand through his hair. Drew waited for the blond spikes to form, then grinned when they did. "Uh, Battleflag, right?"

"Of course, doofus." Drew laughed, assuming Will was joking, because Will *had* to be joking. The infirmary was only three days ago. But he didn't laugh back. He simply stood there, gazing out at those Santa Ana Mountains.

"So, um, were you guys playing Zombie?" Drew pressed.

Will shrugged. "We were just skating."

"Makes sense," Drew said. "You're not wearing blindfolds, so, duh . . ." She knocked herself on the side of the head, then giggled awkwardly. "Hey, I should bring my board tomorrow. And we can all—"

"Cool!" Henry said. "You could definitely join me after school—Will has a thing, right, Will? But we could go to the skate park."

"Uh, yeah—right." Will rested a foot on his board and began pushing it back and forth, his gaze now lowered. Had he forgotten to take his Levocetirizine?

Drew shot Fonda a wide-eyed glance. *Now what?*

"Uh, Drew, what's that awesome trick you just learned? The Oliver?"

"An ollie." Drew giggled.

"Yeah," Fonda said. "Do you guys know that one?"

"Yep," Henry said, wiping a mess of hair away from his eyes. "I taught it to Will last year."

"You taught it to *me*?" Will laughed. "Nice try, dude, I taught it to *you*."

"Ha! What a lie!"

"You're the one lying!"

Moments later they were chasing each other around the blacktop, throwing sloppy punches and hurling accusations at one another, leaving Drew and Fonda on the sidelines to watch.

"Um, those guys are waiting for us," Fonda told Drew in her loudest speaking voice. "We better go."

"What *guys*?" Drew asked.

Fonda shot Drew a wide-eyed glare. *Work with me here.*

"Oh, *them*," Drew shouted. "Yeah, we should go!" she echoed, even though she wanted to stay until she figured out why Will was acting so weird. But Fonda's tug was insistent. And probably for the best.

Arm in arm, they hurried across the blacktop, and when it was safe to talk, Drew mumbled, "It wasn't supposed to go like that."

"Yeah." Fonda cut a look to the tiny red logo on Drew's shirt. "I know how you feel."

But she didn't know how Drew felt. No one did. Except for Drew's Tupperware, which they eventually found in the dirt.

chapter seven.

FONDA'S ORIGINAL PLAN was to share her brilliant idea with Drew and Ruthie later that night, during their Friday sleepover, but the crows were cawing overhead like anxious gossips. *Tell them before you get to school!* they seemed to beg. *Tell them right now!*

"Let's brand ourselves," she blurted as she smile-waved at the crossing guard. It was the last day of their first week of school, and she was determined to make a name for herself—for all three of them—before the weekend.

"Brand?" Ruthie asked. "Like we're cattle?"

Drew laughed and said, "Mooove over, Avas, here we come!"

They were obviously joking, but the comment didn't

feel funny. It felt like a combat boot kick to the gut. Fonda was trying to pave a path to popularity for them, trying to help them feel like they belonged. Why didn't they care?

Meanwhile, the Avas were a few feet ahead, walking arm in arm toward the campus, fastened together like links on a chain. Their legs were long, tanned, and perfectly synchronized. They were a Venus razor commercial that didn't need color coordinating to prove they moved through life together. It was obvious.

"We should start an Instagram account," Fonda continued. "We'll post live stories from our sleepovers and pictures of us doing fun things. And guess what our hashtag can be?" She unhooked one strap of her backpack, letting it dangle. "Nesties!"

Drew's nose crinkled the way it did when Doug crop-dusted her with a fart. "Actually?"

Fonda nodded. "Next-door besties."

Drew dropped her skateboard to the grass, stomped on its tail, and caught it. "Nappen."

"What's *nappen*?"

"Another word my mom invented. It stands for not gonna happen."

"Wouldn't that be nogoppen?" Ruthie asked.

"Yes, but pointing that out to my mom is nogoppen," Drew said. "I don't want to encourage her."

"That's fine." Ruthie shrugged. "My parents won't let me have a phone anyway, so—"

"And mine won't let me have Instagram," Drew added.

"Then I'll do the posting," Fonda said.

Ruthie finger-combed her bangs. "If we can't see it, what's the point?"

"The point is for other people to know we're a friend group."

"I don't get it. Are friend groups a thing at Poplar? They weren't at Forest Day. Probably because 'social hierarchies' were against the rules, but still—"

"Friend groups were allowed at St. Catherine's, but I wasn't in one. I was more of a floater."

"A *floater*?" Ruthie giggled. "That sounds like something you flush."

Drew cracked up.

Fonda closed her eyes and took three cleansing breaths because crying never solved anything and, with the bell about to ring, there was no time to explain what she thought they already knew. Which was that Fonda was over being overlooked. She wanted to be admired like her sisters, envied like the Avas, and appreciated for helping others live their best lives. When she appeared on campus flanked by two amazing girls who saw in Fonda what no one else had, she assumed others would see it too.

But those two amazing girls weren't seeing Fonda anymore, they were looking in other directions, preoccupied with decoding Will's cryptic behavior and learning through lunch with the Titans. Fonda was finally at school with her besties—but she had never felt more alone.

"The point is," Fonda said, "if people know we exist, we matter, and I want us to matter, okay?"

"Don't we already matter?" Ruthie asked.

"We matter to each other, but we don't matter to anyone else."

"Why does it matter if we matter to anyone else?" Ruthie said. "The only thing that should matter is mattering to each other."

Drew smacked the sides of her helmet where her ears would be and shouted, "Stop saying *matter*! It doesn't sound like a real word anymore."

Ruthie laughed. "That happens to me with the word *pickle*. If I say it too much, the back of my throat locks up, and my lips get all spitty. Wanna see?"

"Who says *pickle* too much?" Drew asked.

"Peter Piper," Ruthie said.

While the two of them laughed, Fonda silently apologized to the gift-wrapped period purses in her backpack. She made them for the girls—a surprise to celebrate the end of their first week at Poplar—but she wasn't about to hand them out when there was nothing to celebrate. Fonda's vision board turned out to be nothing more than a kindergarten collage, her LIKES felt more like HATE, and their official COD was colorblind.

The five-minute bell rang, and the girls headed inside.

"Sleepover at my house tonight," Fonda reminded them.

"Then a movie tomorrow, right?" Drew said. "I mean, it's not like I'll be playing Zombie or anything."

Fonda's chest tightened. Did Drew only want to go to the movies because Will wasn't interested? She felt like a backup plan.

"No movie for me," Ruthie sighed. "I have to hang out with the Titans tomorrow."

"On a Saturday?"

"Who are the Titans?" Drew asked.

"That's what our teacher calls us," Ruthie said as they parted ways. "Don't get me started."

"Don't get me stah-ted," Drew said mournfully.

Fonda wanted to put an arm around her and squeeze. She wanted to say, for the thousandth time that week, *Forget Will. You deserve a five-star guy with a ten-star heart. Let's find one.* But her spirit was too weak to lift anyone up, too dark to shed light. Unlike Drew, Fonda hadn't been rejected by a boy she'd spoken to once; Fonda had been rejected by two girls she'd known forever.

Cleansing breaths were no match for this kind of surge. This was bigger than that. Much, much bigger.

"Running to pee," she managed. "Meet you in class."

Inside the bathroom, Fonda hotfooted to the last stall and slammed the door behind her. Why didn't Drew and Ruthie understand? Fonda knew they thought she was just being shallow, but maybe that was because she had been forced to wade in the kiddie pool her whole life while her sisters surfed the Pacific—literally and metaphorically. This was supposed to be Fonda's year. The year she got noticed, the year she was going to *be* someone. She'd made such a good plan, but no one would follow it. Was it because they thought it was silly? Or were they just so busy with their new lives, they couldn't be bothered? Fonda didn't know which was worse—knowing that Drew and Ruthie rejected her ideas or the possibility of them moving on without her. The tears came fast after that last thought, dribbling down her cheeks and colliding with the sides of her nose. Even they were discombobulated.

Finally, when Fonda was drained and tired, she dabbed her eyes with coarse toilet paper and steadied her breath. But the crying sounds continued . . .

Was there someone in the stall next to her?

Fonda peeked under the gap and found a pair of tanned legs, gold sandals, and a girl with problems of her own.

"Are you okay?"

"Not really," she sniffled.

Fonda stepped out of the stall. "What is it?"

"Trust me, you don't want to know."

"I do!" Fonda said. The best way to forget her own problems was to meddle in someone else's. "Really."

The final bell rang.

"No! I can't go out there," said the trembling voice.

"I get it," Fonda said. "Out there sucks."

The girl offered a thin laugh and the stall door clicked open. It was Ava R. The shirt that had previously been tucked into her white shorts now hung loose around her hips.

"What happened?" Fonda asked, as if they bathroom-chatted on the daily.

Ava R. turned to reveal blood on the back of her shorts.

Fonda widened her eyes. "Did you just—"

A fresh batch of tears arrived on the scene.

"First time?"

Ava R. nodded.

Fonda pulled her in for a hug. Yes, to offer comfort, but also because she heard periods were contagious and she desperately wanted to catch one. "The first time is really scary," she said, leaving out the fact that her statement was hearsay, not personal experience.

"Was yours like this?" Ava R. pointed to the stain on her shorts.

"Worse." Fonda bit her lip. She didn't typically like to lie, but desperate times . . . "It was a crime scene."

"What did you do?"

Hmmmm . . . Fonda glanced down at the beige tiles. *What* did *I do?* She quickly put herself in Ava R.'s situation, and . . . *Bam!* She knew exactly what she'd do. "I used my period purse."

"Your what?"

Fonda unzipped her backpack and removed one of the tissue-wrapped bags with a flourish. "Open it."

Ava R. peeled off the gold paper and grinned. "It matches my shorts," she said of the white-and-red polka-dotted cosmetics bag.

"I picked that pattern on purpose."

"Makes sense." Ava R. smiled that toothy selfie smile of hers. Unlike Fonda, who probably had soggy Chihuahua face, Ava R. wore emotional breakdowns well. Her ducts didn't puff; they glistened. And her wide, photogenic face wasn't the least bit splotchy. She was every bit the blond-haired, brown-eyed beauty she always was. But vulnerable. Which made her even more annoyingly attractive. "So, what does a period purse *do*?"

"It holds everything a girl needs when she's caught off guard."

"Actually?"

"Actually." Fonda beamed.

"Oh my g-haud, thank you! I'll return it tomorrow, I promise."

"Keep it," Fonda said. "I have a bunch."

Before she knew it, Ava R. wrapped her in a vanilla-scented hug and squeezed. "Fonda, you are the absolute best."

Just like that, the boulder of emotions pressing down on her chest disintegrated. Ava R. knew her name. Ava R. said she was the absolute best. Ava R. thought she, and her period purse, mattered. It may have taken seven years for Fonda to get noticed, but the wait suddenly seemed worth it.

As Fonda dashed off to class, she thought of the fortune glued to the top of her vision board and giggled with delight. Her golden opportunity had finally arrived, and it was red.

chapter eight.

"SWEETHEART, YOUR FRIENDS are here!" Ruthie's mom called from the kitchen.

The carrot-orange TAG van was parked in front of her house, and while it was full of kids her age, they most certainly were not her friends. Ruthie's friends were going to a movie because it was Saturday and that's what nesties did. But Ruthie didn't feel like a nestie anymore. She was a lestie now—a left-out nestie— who had to fake laugh when Fonda and Drew made fun of their science teacher's turtle ties. Not that Ruthie didn't think turtle ties were eyesores, she did! It was that their stories about classes and teachers and lunch gardens were hard to relate to because most of their jokes were had-to-be-theres, and Ruthie was always somewhere else. Not only did the Titans learn through lunch, they learned through weekends too, and who wanted to talk about *that*? Suddenly, being gifted had become the kind of *gift* Ruthie wanted to return.

"Over here!" Sage waved, indicating the open seat beside her. She was dressed in her usual garb, all black with gold sneakers, because she, like Steve Jobs, didn't want to waste brain cells choosing clothes.

The van turned onto the 405 freeway and headed north. Apparently, every time they went on a field trip, someone new got to make the playlist. Today it was Favian's turn, and he had chosen *Hamilton*. He knew every word of the musical, and so did everyone else by now because he was either playing it, rapping it, or talking about it. All week, Ruthie thought his obsession was annoying, but now, with everyone singing along, it felt kind of festive.

Just then, Rhea shut off the stereo and grabbed the intercom above the driver. She was wearing a Titans T-shirt, which she promised they would all have by their next field trip. It was a promise Ruthie hoped she would break. What was it with Poplar? Why was everyone trying to dress the same?

"Today we're going to learn how to think under pressure and work as a team," she announced.

The Titans cheered.

"See if you can figure out where we're going from the following riddle."

"She always does this." Sage pulled a notebook from her backpack and click-clicked her pen. "It's super cool, am I right?"

"You're trapped in a forest with four exits," Rhea began. "One to the north, south, east, and west. There's a swarm of poisonous insects guarding the north exit. There's a massive hole by the west exit that's too wide to cross, even by rope. Lions who haven't eaten in three months are at the south exit. And the east exit is blocked by an enormous stone slab that's impossible to climb. Which exit do you choose?"

"South," Ruthie blurted.

"Seriously?" Sage whispered. "Have you heard this before?"

"No."

"Then how did you—"

"Explain yourself," Rhea said, giving nothing away.

"The lions haven't eaten in three months, correct?"

Rhea nodded.

"Then they're dead."

"Precisely!" Rhea said. "Your reasoning is sound, and your speed was impressive." She began to applaud, and much to Ruthie's surprise, the Titans applauded with her. Not in the slow, measured way of jealous types. These claps were hearty, robust, supportive. In other words, confusing. It wasn't that they had been mean all week, but with the exception of Sage, they hadn't been exactly *friendly*.

"Based on that riddle, who can guess where we're going?" Rhea asked.

"Zoo!"

"Insect farm?"

"Ropes course!"

"Camping."

"In-N-Out Burger."

"No." Rhea smiled. "We're going to an escape room."

Everyone cheered, but no one louder than Ruthie. Mission Xpossible was a local attraction where a "team" got locked in a room, usually with some kind of theme, and they had to find clues and solve puzzles in order to get out. Ruthie, being an escape room record holder, was just fifteen X-cape points shy of winning a rice cooker. But more importantly, if she could lead the Titans to freedom in under forty minutes, she'd get back in time to meet Drew and Fonda for the movie. Win-win, fit-it-all-in!

As the bus pulled into the Mission Xpossible parking lot, Ruthie humbly let Sage know that she was a record holder and asked if she wanted any tips. To which Sage replied, "Everyone, quiet! Ruthie has an announcement to make!"

Ruthie slid down the back of her seat. *"What are you doing?"* she hissed, cheeks burning from the heat of too much attention.

"I'm trying to help you help us," Sage whispered back. Then to the group, "Hey, everyone, Ruthie is fifteen points away from the rice cooker. She knows how to—"

"Save it for the room," Rhea said, flashing her palm. "The goal here is to work together under pressure. No planning or strategizing before you get in there. Got it?"

"Got it." Ruthie nodded. Then she turned to Sage and whispered, "Thanks a lot."

"You're welcome." Sage beamed.

"I was being sarcastic."

"I wasn't."

Ruthie cocked her head. "Huh?"

"Everyone knows this is about breaking records. And when we do, Rhea will know it's because of you. So, yeah, you're welcome." Sage shrugged like it was no big deal. "You'd do the same for me, am I right?"

Ruthie's insides flushed with the kind of warmth one feels when they realize they've made a new friend, because that was X-actly the kind of thing real friends did . . .

"I would," she said, meaning it.

"Good!" Sage said, grabbing Ruthie by the sleeve of her ice cream cone sweatshirt. "Now let's go crack some codes!"

The Titans were greeted by a heavily pierced college-aged boy who, after blindfolding them, led the group into a room that smelled like cleaning products.

"The objective is simple," he said. "Locate the golden challis and escape with it in under an hour. Ready . . . ?"

When the buzzer sounded, they whipped off their

blindfolds to find they were in a messy janitor's closet. Bottles of bleach had been turned over, mops were on the ground, and the shelves were crooked.

"Gross," said Tomoyo.

"I think they forgot to clean up after the last group," offered Alberta.

"It's not a hotel room," said Conrad.

"Meaning?"

"There's no maid service."

"It's supposed to look this way," Ruthie said. "The clock is ticking. Fan out and look for clues." More than teamwork and escape times, she wanted to get back before Fonda and Drew left for the movie.

Sage cleaned her glasses and rolled up her sleeves. She was ready to work. "What kind of clues?"

"A code, a key, a lock. Look under tables and shelves—" Ruthie paused when she spotted Quinn, who was on his knees unscrewing one of the socket plates from the wall. "That's a dead end. Try something else." Ruthie knew she was being a little short, but every minute wasted was a minute apart from her nesties.

"How do you know?"

"Light switches, socket plates, smoke detectors . . .

they're part of the room, not the set. Try straightening those shelves and see if it triggers anything. Sometimes the clues are on paper," Ruthie added. "Favian, check the stack of employee punch cards. Everest, you're on broom handles and detergent jugs. Quinn, see if there's a black-light flashlight. Conrad, open the books."

"Why?"

"To see if any are hollowed out," Sage said, getting it. "There might be a clue inside."

"I found a clipboard with a photograph on it!" Alberta called. "It's a shot of this room, only clean."

"Lemme see," Ruthie said, swiping it. Photographs often held valuable clues. "Everyone, make this place look exactly like it does in the picture."

They hurried about, banging into one another while Ruthie barked orders.

"Would it kill her to say please?" Conrad huffed.

Ruthie ignored the dig, determined to stay the course.

"Now what?" asked Tomoyo once the room was clean.

Ruthie surveyed their work, shocked that they still

didn't have a lead. Then she noticed the crooked punch clock behind Conrad and said, "Straighten that."

With an indignant sigh, he nudged it into place. One of the walls slid open to reveal a warehouse filled with packing crates.

"Yes!" Ruthie shouted. If they kept up this pace, she, Fonda, and Drew would be dipping their popcorn in nacho cheese sauce in time to see the trailers. "Follow me," she told Sage. "I've got this."

Together they zipped around their classmates, cracking codes, turning keys, and busting locks. At minute thirty-four, they found the challis in crate #27 and managed to set a new record that earned the Titans free pizza in the party room and Ruthie a brand-new Zojirushi rice cooker.

"Congratulations, TAG'ers," Rhea enthused. "You hold the record for fastest escape at Mission Xpossible! Titans Are . . ." She paused, clearly hoping for a suitable G-word, but no one responded.

"Titans Are . . ." Rhea called, trying again.

Zandra broke the silence. "Greedy. Titans Are Greedy."

"Grabby," Alberta said. "Titans Are Grabby."

"Garrulous," Tomoyo said.

Sage tapped a quick note on her phone and showed it to Ruthie. *How about Gealous?*

Ruthie looked back at the building, confused. What was happening here? They'd just busted out of an escape room in record time. Now everyone was free to get on with their weekend plans. Wasn't that something to celebrate? Shouldn't their G-word have been *Grateful*?

"Am I missing something here?" Rhea asked.

Quinn raised his hand. "Ruthie and Sage took over and iced everyone out."

"And it's a good thing we did," Sage said. "Or we never would have won."

"This was supposed to be about teamwork, not winning!" Tomoyo said.

"Yeah, well, it wasn't!" Conrad told Rhea.

"I see your point, but—"

"I learn by doing, not obeying," Alberta said. "And they were—"

"That's enough," Rhea said. "Now, everyone in the van. Silently, please."

Ruthie could feel the heat from their resentful glares as they boarded. She could hear their judgy whispers while they claimed their seats. She hadn't meant to hurt anyone's feelings, and she felt bad that she had. But they performed under pressure and worked as a team. They won! Wasn't that the point?

"It appears as though we have a TM on our hands," Rhea said into the intercom as they pulled out of the parking lot.

"A what?" Ruthie whispered to Sage.

"Teachable moment," Sage whispered back.

"I made this about teamwork, yes," she continued, "but every team needs a leader in order to achieve their goals. And what was your goal?"

No one spoke.

"What. Was. Your. Goal?"

"To escape as fast as we could," Sage offered.

"And did you accomplish that?"

"Yes," Sage answered.

"And did Ruthie's instincts and experience contribute to that?"

"Big-time," Sage said.

Ruthie wanted to hug her new friend but sat on her hands instead.

"Then why isn't everyone thanking her for leading

you to victory?" Rhea asked. "Your egos are getting the best of you, that's why." She paused to let them take this in. "You were right, this exercise was about teamwork, and yet, most of you were out for individual glory. Each of you wanted to be the hero, but no one gets to be a hero by wanting it. You get to be a hero by transcending your ego and doing what needs to be done, whether anyone notices or not. Think about it . . ."

Ruthie wanted to spring to her feet and applaud her teacher's evolved approach. But she thought it best to stay seated on her hands and stare out the window amidst the suffocating silence like everyone else.

After they dropped her off, Ruthie ran up the steps to Fonda's house and triple rang the bell.

Amelia answered the door wearing a yellow bikini top and jeans. "She's at Drew's."

Ruthie bolted over to the Hardens' and triple rang again. Then she knocked an *R* in Morse code for some added oomph.

Drew's brother opened the door and just kind of looked at her. "Why aren't you at the movies with Drew and Fonda?"

"So, they left?"

He took a bite of an energy bar. "Yeah. Like twenty minutes ago."

All that work, all that drama, and her friends were already gone.

"Sorry, dude," Doug said, chewing as he shut the door.

Ruthie glanced down at her new Zojirushi and began to cry. She didn't even like rice.

chapter nine.

DREW DIPPED A piece of popcorn in the nacho cheese and tossed it in her mouth. Hot processed goo with a hint of jalapeño, followed by a satisfying crunch. It was a five-star taste sensation that dropped to a four because Ruthie wasn't there holding the plastic container, which had always been her thing.

Fonda unwrapped a pink Starburst. "We hung out more when she was at Forest Day."

"Yeah, I think Poplar Middle School is cursed," Drew said. Then she laughed a little. "Get it? PMS is cursed."

"No."

Drew felt a wash of disappointment. Fonda always got her jokes. Maybe Ruthie was right. That straight hair was making her more serious.

"You told me Winfrey calls her period 'the curse,' and the school's initials are PMS, so . . ."

"Oh, yeah." Fonda smiled. "Why didn't I think of that?"

The bigger question should have been *How had she thought of it?* Will had taken up so much space in her brain lately, it was a miracle she still had room for random musings. "I think he has prosopagnosia."

Fonda grabbed a handful of popcorn. "Who?"

"Will."

"What *is* prosop—" Fonda said.

"Face blindness. It's a neurological disorder where the sufferer has a hard time recognizing people. The camp nurse told me about it," Drew said with a dip of her popcorn. "Do you think Will has it and she was trying to warn me without actually warning me?"

"Maybe. Or what if . . ." Fonda paused. "Forget it."

"What?"

"Nothing."

"Tell me!"

Fonda put the bucket of popcorn on the empty seat beside her. "Maybe he doesn't have propaganda."

"Prosopagnosia."

"Whatever. That's not my point."

"Then what?" Drew asked, eager for Fonda's response. She always gave great advice and might have had an explanation for Will's sudden change of heart—something Drew hadn't already considered.

"My point is," Fonda said with an exhausted sigh, "maybe you're too good for him."

"I'm too good, so he doesn't like me? How does that make sense? Wouldn't me being good make him like me even more?"

Fonda placed a hand on Drew's shoulder. "Will isn't the one saying you're too good. I am."

"Ugh!" Drew knocked her head against the back of her seat. "I don't get any of this!"

"It's not enough for a guy to be nice to you one day, then all ignore-y the next. He needs to be nice every day. And if he's not, and you're not doing anything about it, I have to protect you." Fonda reached for a handful of popcorn, tilted back her head, and released it into her mouth. "Basically"—she chewed—"if we're going to honor our fifth-grade pact and only crush on

boys who get three thumbs up—one from each of us—
Will has got to go."

Fonda's words hurt like a dozen arrows to the
heart. Was Fonda making her choose? "I know he was
acting weird, but there's a reason for it. I just have to
figure it out."

"No, what you *need* to figure out is why you're
letting a boy treat my best friend like a Christmas
stocking."

"Huh?"

"A once-a-year hang."

Drew, too stubborn to laugh, pressed her lips
together.

"I just don't get it," Fonda said, her eyes fixed on
the movie screen, an ad for job opportunities at Regal
Cinemas.

"Get what?"

"You deserve a Hemsworth brother. And you're settling for someone who isn't even nice," Fonda said, her
light brown eyes wide with sincerity. "Why Will? Why do
you like him so much?"

Drew reached for the end of her ponytail and
twirled. She had several reasons, actually:

1. They had a five-star infirmary chat.

2. They both skated and played Zombie.

3. They loved to make fun of *The Skateboard Kid.*

4. Will's eyes were the same color blue as Drew's dress-up jeans.

5. They were the exact same height.

But Drew already told Fonda that, so all she said was "Why wouldn't I?"

"For one thing," Fonda said, "do you really want to crush on a guy who can't remember your face?"

"There are hacks," Drew said, thinking of Grandma Mae.

When she got dementia, Grandpa Lou left sticky-note reminders all over the house. *Keep screen door closed so Tabasco doesn't get out. Tabasco is our dog. The password on your phone is 7131. The mailman's name is Roland. He is kind.* It wasn't ideal, but it wasn't impossible either.

"All I'm saying is, never let a guy be responsible for your happiness."

"I'm not," Drew said. "He's responsible for my unhappiness."

Fonda turned back to the screen. "Bottom line? Find a crush who's worthy of you. Move on."

Drew bristled. *Move on?* She wasn't a lamp. She couldn't turn all that electricity off with the flick of a switch. And for some reason, Fonda didn't get that. She didn't get *her*. She used to, but she didn't anymore. If only Ruthie had been there. Maybe she would have understood that when Drew's heart and brain disagreed, her heart always won. Even when it didn't have proof or evidence or facts to back it up, whether it was right or not, it didn't matter. Hearts weren't smart, but they screamed louder than logic. And Drew's screaming heart could shatter glass.

With that, she turned to Fonda, ready to explain all this to her, when at the exact same time, Fonda said, "I'm sorry. I'm not trying to be harsh. I just want you to be happy, and this whole Will thing is making you seriously un. Maybe you need a distraction."

Just then, two boys settled into the seats behind them.

"Well, hello, distractions," Fonda muttered.

"Seriously?"

"Yes. Delete Will from your crush cart and add—"
She hitched her thumb in their general direction.

There she was, being treated like a lamp again. Or a
computer: enter a new name and replace all.

"I don't even know who they are."

"Yes, you do," Fonda whispered. She leaned forward toward the fallen Starburst wrappers and sig-
naled for Drew to do the same. Then, "They go to
Poplar. Jasper is in our English class, and I have PE
with Frankie." Fonda raised her eyebrows. "Will you
at least try?"

"Stop saying his name," Drew told her.

Fonda rolled her eyes.

"Fine." Drew grinned. It was easier than arguing.

Fonda made the introductions just as Jasper was
taking a bite of his hot dog.

"Hey." He chewed, oblivious to the smear of
ketchup on his thumb.

"Hey," Frankie echoed as he rested his feet a little
too close to Fonda's face. His hair looked like ramen
noodles before the water was added.

"You play water polo, right?" Drew asked, feeling

surprisingly bold. It was easy to be confident when she didn't care.

"Yeah," he said suspiciously. "How'd you know?"

"Yeah," Fonda asked. "How *did* you know?"

"My brother, Doug, used to play. His hair went all haywire too. It's the chlorine."

"Are you calling my hair haywire?"

"So, Jasper," Fonda said, taking over, "have you started reading *The Outsiders* yet?"

"Nah. I'll watch the movie instead," he said, wiping his ketchupy thumb on his surf trunks.

"Same," said Frankie.

"Big mistake," Drew said. "The movie is a snoozer compared to the book."

"Oh yeah?" Jasper leaned forward. "Maybe you can read it to me sometime."

Frankie laughed. Drew did not. What if Jasper had a low Lexile score and needed help reading? That wasn't funny; it was sad.

The theater lights dimmed, and the girls turned to face the screen.

"See?" Fonda said. "It helps talking to other boys, right?"

Drew wanted to say that it didn't help at all. That all roads, both imaginary and real, led to Will. But Fonda looked so pleased with herself for solving Drew's problem, she didn't have the heart to tell her the truth, so all she said was "Yep. I'm totally over him."

"How over?"

"Soooo over," Drew managed.

Fonda rolled her wrist, wanting more.

"Like if Will was lying on the side of the road with a bunch of broken bones, I'd make like a chicken and cross. I'm done with that doozer."

"Dude loser?" Fonda guessed.

"Yep." Drew nodded. "Done."

"Really?" Fonda beamed, clearly proud.

"Really."

But while Drew's imaginary self was crossing the road, her real self was crossing her fingers.

chapter ten.

THE CALIFORNIA SUN was searing Fonda's scalp. Her banging heart was begging for mercy. But ever since she gave Ava R. that period purse, PE, and all the misery that went with it, may as well have stood for Popularity Express, because now she was searing and huffing alongside the Avas, which lessened the trauma considerably.

"Let's talk party list," said Ava G. in that girly, high-pitched voice of hers. "I want everyone's top ten."

They were trudging up the first of three painfully steep trails on what Coach Pierce referred to as a "Superhike." Everyone else called it a "Superhurl" because someone always lost their lunch by the end.

Typically, Fonda dreaded the monthly outing. All

those sweaty kids in matching maroon uniforms, panting and pushing to the front as if "speedy hill walker" was a fast-track to Harvard. At least her legs had grown an inch since last year, but she still had to walk double time to keep up.

"No fair," panted Ava H. as she gathered her long brown curls and tossed them over her shoulder. "You always. Do. This."

"Do. What?"

"Ask us questions. Right as we start. Going up. The hill."

"You're right." Ava R. laughed. "She does. Do. That. It's so. Unfair."

"Why. Un. Fair?" Fonda panted, daring to insert herself in the conversation.

"That. Way. We do. All. The. Talking when we're going. Uphill. And she gets to breathe. And. Listen."

"Un. Fair?" Ava G. said. "Or brilliant?"

They only half laughed, due to their limited oxygen. But Fonda didn't hold back. The joy she got from mattering to the Avas was all the oxygen she needed. Not that she wanted to join their group. She wanted her own group, one where members had different names and unique hairstyles. But Ruthie was busy with the Titans, and Drew, who claimed to be over Will, was still watching him, all moony, every chance she got.

Now, as Fonda trudged up the hill, she couldn't help wondering if Drew and Ruthie were moving on without her. Because it certainly felt that way. On top of everything else, neither one of them wished her a happy half birthday that morning, which was weird, because they always celebrated halves. Did they not remember? Or worse, did they remember and not even care? Maybe Drew was upset that Fonda gave it to her straight at the movies, but Will *was* acting like a doozer. And weren't friends supposed to tell each other the truth? They always had before.

"Back to. The list," Ava G. said, fanning her glistening forehead. "Who do you want to invite? My parents said I can have. Thirty people. So, we each. Get. Ten."

"My list is gonna be post office," said Ava H.

"Huh?"

"All male!"

Fonda laughed with the rest of them, like she could totally relate. But on the inside, she was spiraling. It wasn't like Fonda was anti-guy or anything. She'd had a few mild crushes and certainly noticed if a boy looked handsome. But she couldn't name three she wanted to have at a party, let alone ten. Was something majorly wrong with her?

The girls began reciting their lists, and Fonda did her best to listen. But their legs were long, and hers were only medium. Matching their pace was becoming difficult, and she was lagging behind. All she heard was:

"I can't stand ____ smell of Axe ____ spray."

And "I'm not going to ____ anyone with chapped lips. I might as well ____ with a nail file."

And "Can we ____ back to the list?"

"Fine. I want Jess, Jack P. ___ ack H. Ja ___ C. ____ Reef, Lu ____, Dutch ____ Gr____ . . ."

It was like being on a phone call with bad reception. Words, sounds, and sometimes complete sentences dropped off. But one thing was clear: Fonda hadn't heard her name on any of their lists. Not even Ava R.'s. The bathroom talk, the period purse . . . it was all for nothing. No matter what Fonda did, it was never enough. And now, because of her, Drew and Ruthie wouldn't be enough either. They'd always be seen as the girls who didn't make the cut. Sure, they could still start a friend group, but no one would join. And when no one wanted in, you were out.

"Tighten your abs, and let's pick up the pace!" called Coach Pierce as they began climbing the third and final hill.

Fonda did no such thing.

Why scramble to keep up when the Avas proved that keeping up was impossible? *Giving up* was Fonda's speed now.

As she shuffled along the dusty trail, kicking up dirt and resentments, Fonda was overcome by dizziness. Green cactuses, dry brown brush, buzzing bees, heavy breathing, and occasional whiffs of body odor swirled into a stew of sensory overload and churned something deep inside her stomach.

Saliva rushed her mouth.

Her body burped without permission.

Then up came her chicken taquitos.

"Superhurl!" shouted Frankie, the boy with ramen noodle hair.

And just like that, Fonda Miller was no longer invisible. The image of her wiping spittle from her mouth would be etched in the brains of twenty-three kids for all eternity.

chapter eleven.

IT WAS THURSDAY night, but the pit of loneliness in Ruthie's stomach was Sunday strong. She was starting to dread school, resent it even, because school had turned her into a social refugee, leaving her to wander with no place to call home.

Yes, Ruthie had the Titans, and double yes, she was learning oodles of fun facts from Rhea. For example: the word *algebra* comes from the ancient Arabic word *al-jabr*, which means the "reunion of broken parts." As in "Ruthie, Drew, and Fonda need an al-jabr." But all this learning through lunch, delicious as it was, meant Drew and Fonda were making memories without her. And Ruthie couldn't possibly find joy in perfect test scores when she was falling behind with her friends.

Now, as she completed chapter three of her creative writing assignment, her insides swirled with a restless sort of discontent. Her story, "Foxie the Werefox," was about a seventh-grade girl who transitioned into a fox during the full moon, and like the tights that shredded when she shape-shifted, Foxie was torn. Being forced to hunt squirrels and survive in the wild was exhilarating, but doing it alone was isolating. In this chapter, she discovered an elixir that had the power to turn her back into a regular girl. If she drank it, Foxie would never feel that exhilaration again. If she didn't, she'd have nothing in common with her friends, and they'd move on without her. By the end of the chapter, Foxie found herself in a lose-lose situation and decided to sleep on it.

After a quick proofread, Ruthie uploaded the assignment to the TAG website, feeling just as confused as that poor werefox. She, the author, was responsible for getting Foxie out of that pickle, but if Ruthie knew how to do that, she wouldn't be dealing with the same conundrum in her own life.

"Hey." Her mother smiled softly as she pushed open the door of Ruthie's bedroom. Her contacts were out; her glasses and sweatpants were on. It was Ruthie's favorite look. It meant Dr. Fran wasn't on call. She was home for the night.

"Let's sit," she said, gesturing to the bed.

Ruthie slumped down beside her.

"How's everything going?" Fran asked, the two lines between her eyebrows deep with concern.

"Fine. Why?"

"I read the latest chapter of 'Foxie the Werefox' on the parent portal and—"

"Already? I just posted it."

Fran placed her hand on Ruthie's knee the way she did when a sick toddler was afraid. No wonder parents raved about her bedside manner on Yelp. Heat spilled from her touch; empathy radiated from her hazel eyes. Your pain was her pain. She was all in. "I'm worried about Foxie. She seems . . . conflicted."

Ruthie sighed, relieved this wasn't about her. "She *is* conflicted."

"About what?"

Ruthie looked through her mother's glasses and deep into her eyes. *Really? You can't figure it out?* "Either her brain is happy, or her heart is happy. They're never both happy at the same time."

Fran laughed weakly.

"What's so funny?"

"You just described the struggle of a working mother."

"I did? How?"

"If I'm with my patients, I can't be with you. If I'm with you, I can't help my patients. Being with one means disappointing the other. It's a very hard balance to strike."

"How do you deal with it?"

"I do the best I can when I'm at work and the best I can when I'm with you and Dad."

"But if you had to choose one, which would it be?"

"I'd choose my heart. I'd choose *you*."

"So you think Foxie should drink the elixir and become human again?"

"That depends," Fran said. "Is Foxie having a hard time adjusting to her new . . . uh, hunting lifestyle?"

"Adjusting?"

"Yes. It's a big change from her old life. Maybe it's overwhelming her. In which case, she should be patient. She'll get used to it in time."

"She doesn't have time. That's the problem. Her friends aren't nocturnal. They're on a totally different schedule. She'll never see them, and they'll move on without her."

"Well, maybe Foxie will make new friends. Werefox friends, like her."

"She doesn't want werefox friends. She wants her regular friends."

"More than she wants to hunt and chase squirrels?"

"Yes."

"Then Foxie should drink the elixir."

"She should?"

"Absolutely. Why keep her in a situation she can't handle?"

Ruthie felt a pinch of defensiveness on Foxie's behalf. Of course she could *handle* it. She just missed her friends.

"I'm no writer," Fran continued, "but I do know

there's a difference between what a character wants and what a character *needs*. For example, Foxie may *want* to stay a werefox because it's exciting, but she may *need* to be with her friends because they make her happy. Get it?"

"Got it!" Ruthie gave her mom a giant hug that knocked them flat onto the bed. Without knowing it, Fran had revealed the code to Ruthie's personal escape room.

Now all she had to do was activate it, open the door, and leave.

chapter twelve.

IT HAD BEEN six days since Drew sat beside Fonda at the movie theater and promised she'd get over Will. And she tried. She really did. Did she still look for him before school, in the halls, during lunch, after school, and when she walked home with Fonda and Ruthie? Yes. She was still human. But when Drew spotted Will, she didn't say hello, didn't wave, didn't even smile. It was progress. It also felt like getting donkey-kicked in the chest.

"Maybe that guy Henry had something to do with it," Drew said as the girls began drifting off to sleep. She was hosting their Friday-night sleepover, which, she decided, entitled her to one minor slip-up.

"Something to do with what?" Fonda asked, flipping her pillow to the cold side.

"Why Will was so strange. I mean, you saw the way Henry looked at Will when I mentioned we'd met at camp. Like it was weird that we already knew each other."

"Who is Henry?" Ruthie mumbled, sounding a little offended. "Why don't I know about him?"

"Henry is Will's friend," Drew said, feeling a little offended herself. She explained all of this weeks ago. "Anyway, maybe Henry is mad that Will didn't tell him he knew me—"

"Why would he be mad about that?"

"I don't know. That's what I'm trying to figure out."

"Hmmm," Ruthie said. Moments later, the sound of their collective breathing took over, which was not ideal. If they fell asleep without solving this, it would be morning the next time they spoke. Drew would no longer be hosting their sleepover, and her slip-up opportunity would be over.

"I was thinking of skating at the school tomorrow. If he's there playing Zombie, do you think I should say hi or ignore him?"

No one answered.

"I mean, I don't want him to think I'm still into him. I'm not. But at the same time—"

"Dude!" Fonda snapped.

Drew smiled. Finally, some enthusiasm. "I'm onto something, right?"

"The only thing you're onto is my last nerve."

"Mean," Ruthie said sleepily.

"No, Ruthie, *mean* is letting our friend torture herself over some guy who isn't worth it."

"What if he *is* worth it and he's just being . . . weird?" Drew asked.

"When someone shows you who they are, believe them."

"I *am* believing him," Drew said, thinking back to her five reasons. "I'm believing he's fun."

"But he hasn't been fun. He's been weird. You said so yourself."

"I didn't mean he *is* weird. I meant he was *acting* weird. There's a difference."

Fonda lay back down and covered her head with her pillow. "I give up. I'm going to bed."

Drew lay there staring at the ceiling for so long the glow-in-the-dark stickers she, Ruthie, and Fonda had stuck there when they were eight began to lose their glow. There was more to her story with Will. Drew knew it the way she knew that with practice, she could keep up with Doug at the skate park or that she wanted to be a nurse one day. There was a quiet, confident hum inside her that just knew.

What she didn't know was why her friends kept doubting her. Why they couldn't trust her enough to know it too.

♥

"ARE YOU OKAY?" Drew asked Fonda the following morning as they said their goodbyes on the front porch. The sky was filled with dolphin-colored clouds. The air, with awkwardness.

"Yeah. Why wouldn't I be?"

"I dunno," Drew said, because she didn't. All she did know was that Fonda's brown eyes were distant as she twisted her friendship bracelets around her wrist. "You're both leaving. Usually we go to a movie or bike into town or—"

"I have homework," Ruthie said. "I'm building 3-D models of the diatomic molecules, so it won't actually *feel* like work, but still. There are seven of them, so it's a lot."

"And I have that Obstacles Facing Feminists lecture with my mom."

Drew sighed. It felt like she was getting ignored by Will all over again. Only this wasn't Will; it was her best friends. Sure, every now and then one of them had a Saturday obligation, but both? Never.

"Bummer," Drew mumbled.

Fonda shrugged. "I guess."

I guess? How could going to a lecture *not* be a bummer when they could be at the bead store making necklaces or sipping hot chocolate while deciding which famous people the coffee shop customers resembled? Instead they were parting ways.

Again.

♥

"FLIP UP!" DOUG shouted, thirty minutes later. His light brown hair had been moussed into a "natural" mess, and he was wearing new board shorts, no shirt. Drew didn't bother telling him Winfrey wasn't home, that Joan had taken her girls to the university for the Feminist Fall Lecture Series. If he knew, he'd head to the beach, leaving Drew to spend Saturday alone. And today, not even her favorite medical diagnosis show on Netflix could cheer her up. She needed companionship and a skateboard, stat.

"I *am* flipping up."

"You're not! You're flipping down."

"Lies!" Drew told him. "Watch!" She pressed the ball of her back foot against the tail of her board, dragged the toe of her front foot and jumped. Then she fell on her butt and kicked her board toward Ruthie's driveway. She groaned. She'd locked that trick months ago. What was happening?

"That's not a flip up," Doug said, "It's a flip *out*. What's going on with you?"

When Drew didn't answer, he tossed a pebble at her shoe. When she didn't answer again, he tossed a handful.

"What the heck?"

Lying down beside her, Doug folded his hands under his head like he was on a chaise, not a cul-de-sac of despair. "Come on, tell me."

"Tell you what?"

"Why you've been moping around all morning."

The hair on his arms was golden, same as the stubble on his chin. "Is it girl stuff or boy stuff?"

"Girl stuff."

His cheeks flushed pink. "Oh. Then talk to Mom."

"Not *that* kind of girl stuff." Drew giggled. "It's girl stuff about boy stuff."

"In that case, shoot." Doug sat up and rubbed his hands together.

First, Drew told him about Will and the five reasons why she cared, then braced herself for the part of the story that made her chest tighten. "Then, when I saw him at school, he acted like we'd never met."

"Was he with his buddies?"

"One."

"And you?"

"Just Fonda."

Doug jumped to his feet. "That explains it."

"You think he has an issue with Fonda?"

"No." He pulled Drew up to stand. "It doesn't matter who you were with. The point is you weren't alone, which explains why he was acting cool."

"He wasn't acting cool, Doug. He was acting uncool."

"I meant cool like cold, not cool like me." He winked. "There's a difference."

"Winking is not cool."

"Said the girl hanging out with her brother on a Saturday afternoon."

Drew swatted him on the arm.

"When I left St. Andrew's and went to public, I was a mess too. It takes time to figure everything out."

"Great. So what have you figured out?" Drew asked, aware of the impatience in her own voice. "Besides the fact that *I'm* a mess."

"I figured out that . . ." Doug drummed his thighs to heighten the anticipation.

Drew swatted him again. "Just tell me!"

"Will isn't weird; he's shy. Bam!" Doug jumped back like he always did when he dropped some truth. As if giving it room to land.

"Shy?"

"Yes, shy. Shy and nervous. Guys are terrified of embarrassing themselves in front of girls. And they're even more terrified of embarrassing themselves in front of their buddies."

"Why?" Drew asked, wondering how one could

possibly be embarrassed around their friends. Fonda and Ruthie made her feel better when she did something goofy, not worse. Well, they used to, at least.

"Guys live to torture each other."

"So what am I supposed to do, torture him?"

Doug laughed. "No, the opposite. Find him when he's alone, and see if he's nicer. If he is, don't play games. Be nice back. He needs to know he can trust you. That you won't try to embarrass him. Do that, and you'll be playing Zombie in no time."

"How do you know?"

"Who wouldn't want to shove you off a skate-board?" he teased.

Drew didn't bother asking what to do if he didn't treat her better, because this plan was going to work. It had to work. Where there's a Will, there's a way.

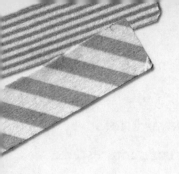

chapter thirteen.

FOOTBALL.

The word was rarely, if ever, spoken by a Miller woman. But with the high school homecoming dance less than a week away, it was all Winfrey and Amelia could talk about. Instead of surfing and playing volleyball, like they usually did on Sundays, they, along with three friends, had transformed the living room into a day spa. To them, "scoring big" meant turning heads on the dance floor after the big game, which they clearly believed would be easier if their pores weren't clogged.

And then there was Fonda. Making popcorn in the kitchen, one kernel at a time, so she could spy on them without appearing to be, well, spying on them. Was it immoral? Probably. But after her failed attempt at forming an influential group, getting left off the Avas' party list, and having a stage-five awkward sleepover with her so-called nesties, Fonda wasn't interested in moral. She was interested in saving her sinking friend-*ships*.

How had everything gone so sideways? When she made her vision board, everything seemed so possible. Probable, even. She could practically *feel* her flat-ironed hair blowing in the breeze as she, Drew, and Ruthie sauntered onto campus, laughing, while the Avas looked on with envy. *How can we be part of their fearless, fashionable, fun-loving group?* their slack jaws would seem to say.

Not only had that not happened, but there she was, yet again, watching her sisters live the life she wanted while hers continued to fall apart. Like the un-popped kernels at the bottom of her bowl, Fonda was there but unwanted. And on top of that, the two people who always treated her like a be-long were acting all so-long.

Was there a little self-pity going on here? No, there

was a lot. Because come on, the sleepover at Drew's was tense because:

1. Fonda lost patience with Drew because she was still hung up on a guy who blew her off.

2. Ruthie heavy-sighed whenever Drew and Fonda shared a story from one of their classes.

3. Drew changed the subject when Ruthie recited a limerick her friend Sage wrote about the periodic table.

4. Fonda was happy that Drew changed the subject, because she was kind of jealous that Ruthie had made a new friend too.

5. Everyone went their separate ways on Saturday, which NEVER happened.

Basically, the next-door besties were acting more like next-door foes, and the idea of changing their name from nesties to noes felt even worse than it sounded.

Fonda would have been lying if she'd said the idea of giving up and moving to Myanmar to build houses for Habitat for Humanity didn't cross her mind. But one of yesterday's speakers at the Feminist Fall Lecture Series talked about the importance of women lifting each other up so they could reach their goals. And that lifted Fonda up. Not enough to keep self-pity at bay, but certainly enough to keep her from moving to Myanmar. Maybe they were going through rough waters, but she was going to right their sinking friend-ship and put the nesties back on course. And if that required a little eavesdropping to find out how the popular girls kept their friend-ships afloat, so be it.

"What's our answer to last year's sneaker pact?" asked Winfrey as she blew on her drying white polish.

"Um, what's the *question*?" muttered her friend Jaymee, the clay on her face mask dried and cracking.

Fonda smiled to herself. Lately, Winfrey had been saying things like *What's our answer to backpacks?* or *What's our answer to beef?* It was her fancy new way of pointing out that a tired old trend needed updating and that she was the person for the job. Basically, it was her "answer" to the normal way of asking, *How can I stand out?* And everyone found it super confusing.

"The question is, we all wore sneakers to the dance

last year, and we need to come up with something better."

That's not a question, Fonda thought. But Winfrey's friends didn't fixate on semantics. Ruthie, on the other hand, would have placed a citizen's arrest.

"Anything but heels." Amelia padded over to the hair-staining station to contemplate the colors. "Like I always say—"

"Cute can be comfortable, and comfortable is cute," everyone said together.

Fonda typed GET A PERSONAL SLOGAN in the Notes app on her phone.

"What about sandals?" said Cami, peeling a crooked false eyelash off her lid.

"Ehhh!" Winfrey said, impersonating an elimination buzzer. "Too daytime."

"Flip-flops?" Priya tried.

"Too July."

"Rain boots?" Jaymee said.

"NF!" Winfrey and Amelia called. It stood for not funny. They shouted it whenever someone told a bad joke.

"I wasn't trying to be funny."

"In your case NF stands for not Filly," Winfrey said.

"Meaning?"

"You don't live in Philadelphia anymore. You live in California. It never rains here. We don't own boots."

Instead of pointing out that *Philly* didn't start with an *F*, the girls fell silent, each of them probably trying to solve the footwear crisis.

"What about no shoes?" Amelia finally said. "A barefoot pact."

Without hesitation, all five girls lifted their bottles of nail polish and clinked, making it official. They would go barefoot to the homecoming dance on Friday. By Saturday everyone would be talking about it. And by Sunday everyone would be doing it. That was how it worked with Fonda's sisters.

And with any luck, that was how it would work with Fonda, Drew, and Ruthie one day.

But how?

Fonda, now hiding under the kitchen table, typed FORM PACTS into her phone when it hit her: next Friday, while her sisters were dancing barefoot at homecoming and the Avas were boy browsing at their party, she would make history with a Sleepover

Spa-tacular. Everything from nail bars to chocolate bars would be available. They could style each other's hair, make DIY face masks, play pin the eyelash on the donkey, create slogans, and form pacts. Not a single NF would be uttered, because everything they said would be hilarious. She would lift the girls up and show them how amazing they were. Prove that they belonged together and that no one—not the Avas, not a doozer, not a time-sucking TAG program, and not even Fonda's sisters—could tear them apart.

chapter fourteen.

EVERY THURSDAY, RHEA quizzed the Titans on the previous week's material to make sure no one was falling behind. It was a gift from the Greek gods, Ruthie thought. The solution to her biggest problem. The key to escaping TAG.

Sticking to the plan, she wrote her final answer: *Newton's first law of motion was force equals mass multiplied by acceleration.* Then she pressed two fingers into her throbbing temple, throbs that were probably tapping *fraud* in Morse code. Because Ruthie knew Newton's first law was "A body in motion stays in motion and a body at rest stays at rest unless acted upon by an unbalanced force." But her goal was to leave, not achieve, so she flubbed her math and English tests too.

The decision to "fail" out of TAG wasn't easy. It involved a detailed pro-con list, followed by a tear-soaked snuggle with Foxie. Gone were the days when Ruthie's biggest decision was whether to hang out with Drew and Fonda at the fro-yo shop or the bead store. Gone were also the days when she could ask them for advice. At least it felt that way. Their last sleepover put the *ugh* in *rough*, and thanks to two TAG field trips and a five-page essay on the importance of civic duty, Ruthie barely saw them all week. At least Fonda's big Spa-tacular sleepover was tomorrow night, but until then, she was forced to problem-solve on her own.

"What do you think of my plan?" Ruthie asked herself.

Depends, she answered. *How many pros? How many cons?*

"Two on each side."

Ugh. That doesn't help.

"My brain says don't do it. It thinks I'll miss the guest speakers, fun facts, and out-of-the-box home-work assignments."

And your heart?

"It says do it."

You don't like those Titans, do you? Are they still gealous of your escape room skills?

"No, they're over it. Everyone is being super nice. Everest even taught me how to sit on my balance ball."

Then why leave?

Ruthie gripped her belly as she considered her response. Just *thinking* about Drew and Fonda moving on without her was nauseating. Because they were more than friends, they were even more than nesties: they were the closest thing to siblings she had. "I'm scared."

Deep down, you know where you belong, Ruthie told herself. *Go with your heart.*

At that, Ruthie hugged Foxie to her chest. She knew what she had to do. And she had just done it.

"Those tests were so easy, am I right?" Sage said now as the Titans filed into the kitchen to grab their lunches from the fridge.

Ruthie nodded, wishing she could tell Sage the truth. She liked Sage, liked that she thought tests were easy too. Because, not to sound braggy, but sometimes Ruthie didn't want to pretend school was hard just to fit in. Sometimes she wanted to complain about how easy it was with someone who might agree.

"Hey, wanna hang out tomorrow night?" Sage asked as they settled in to watch a documentary on climate change.

Ruthie sighed. She would miss learning through lunch. Miss being surrounded by peers who preferred books to the movies, NPR to Netflix, TED Talks to Xbox. Not to mention she was one listen away from knowing the entire *Hamilton* cast album. They were good people. They just weren't *her* people.

"I'd love to, but I have a special spa sleepover tomorrow night," Ruthie said, insides tingling at the thought of sharing her scandalous plan with her girls over hot chocolate and colorful pedicures—that Titans had to maintain a minimum B-plus average to stay in the program, and Ruthie was about to land in the D zone. That Rhea would assume she couldn't handle the material and recommend she leave the program. That they could finally be together!

"Special spa sleepover," Sage echoed. "That's some serious alliteration, am I right?"

"You are indeed." Ruthie laughed. She would miss seeing Sage in class every day. But all she could focus on was the inevitable excitement on Drew's and Fonda's faces when Ruthie told them she threw her test results on purpose.

"Who's having the sleepover?" Sage asked, tucking a strand of pink hair behind her ear. "Alberta?"

"No."

"Tomoyo?"

"No."

"Wait . . . You wouldn't sleep at a boy's house . . . would you?" Sage asked, concerned.

"Ew, no!" Ruthie laughed. She liked knowing that someone other than Drew and Fonda cared enough to wonder who she was hanging out with. "I have two friends outside of TAG."

Sage wrinkled her forehead. "And you still have time to hang out with them?"

I will, Ruthie thought. Because starting Monday, she would be having lunch with Drew and Fonda, sitting in class with Drew and Fonda, and doing homework with Drew and Fonda. Starting Monday, TAG would take on a whole new meaning for Ruthie. It would stand for the Together Always Girls—a program that finally included all three of them.

chapter fifteen.

OPERATION WHERE THERE'S a Will There's a Way was a total bust.

Correction, there was plenty of Will, just no *way* to get him alone. He was always skating with Henry during lunch, and his older sister picked him up after school, so he never walked home. Drew needed a plan B, fast. But Doug worked at the surf shop on Thursdays, the nesties had declared the subject off-limits, and getting advice from her mother was pointless. What did she know about boys?

Sluggish with defeat, Drew finished her home-work, then headed to Green Gates Skate Park to face the bowl. Because when she was dressed in head-to-toe protective pads and peering into a concrete abyss, it was hard to think about unrequited crushes. Surviving the drop was her only thought. That and the fact that she looked like a stormtrooper.

One by one, skaters shot off the lip of the bowl and rounded the turns. The moment Drew saw a break in the action, she put her left foot on the back of the board, bent her knees, shifted her weight forward and plunged.

"Ahhhhhhh!"

Drew had dropped into dozens of pools dozens of times, but she still screamed like she was riding the Silver Bullet at Knott's. Screaming was part of the fun. Everything about skating was part of the fun. Except wiping out, which was rare. But when it did happen, no one judged. Unlike at school, skating mess-ups weren't seen as epic fails. They were opportunities to dust off and try again—and, of course, a chance to use her nursing skills.

As Drew reached the bottom of the bowl, she swiveled her hips to carve, and—*SMASH!* Someone came at her from the left and knocked her to the ground with a heart-stopping thud. Stunned into silence, Drew lay on the concrete in a heap.

Eyes closed, she listened for the wail of ambulance sirens as shadows flickered across her lids. How long before the metallic taste of blood filled her mouth? Before she was hoisted onto a gurney? Before she had to miss Fonda's Sleepover Spa-tacular on account of being dead? That sleepover was supposed to be a do-over. The chance for Drew to actually connect with her friends and have fun, instead of obsessing over Will. Because maybe Fonda and Ruthie were right. Maybe it was time to admit defeat and move on. But if she was dead, how could she possibly—

"Are you okay?" asked a boy. His gravelly voice familiar but strained.

Drew's lids fluttered open to find him leaning over her, shaggy blond hair obstructing his face but not his concern.

"Will?"

Cliché as it seemed, Drew was certain she had died and gone to heaven. Because when a girl spends two and a half weeks trying to talk to a boy and can't make it happen, then suddenly opens her deceased eyes and sees him, heaven is the only thing that makes sense.

"Sorry," he said. "I didn't see you and then I did see you and then—" He clapped his hands together. "Bam!"

Drew scanned his knees for scrapes and abrasions she might have to tend to, but luckily Will was wearing pads.

"Here. Let me help you up."

Will offered his hand. It was warm and soft, not shaky and clammy like Drew's. Once she was back on her feet, he let go, though her body still carried the zing from his touch.

Together, they limped to the nearest bench. Then Will ran to get a bag of ice. Nurse Cate would have been impressed with his bedside manner. But Drew wasn't so sure. Why did it take a near-death experience for Will to acknowledge her? What about that was impressive?

"Who are you here with?" he asked when he got back. He sat beside her and laid his helmet on the bench. "Should I get anyone?"

"I came alone," Drew said, embarrassed. What if he thought she was friendless? "You?"

"Same."

"Oh, good," Drew said. "I mean, sorry."

Will finger-fluffed his hair, which had been flattened by his helmet and held in place by sweat. "I should be apologizing to you."

"For what?" Drew asked, expectant. He was finally going to mention the lunchtime incident.

"Smashing into you."

"Oh, that. It's fine."

He flashed a flirty half smile. "And what are you sorry for?"

"That you don't have any friends," she teased.

"Um." He glanced around. "Neither do you."

"Opposite. I have so many friends Mr. Green Gates had to turn them away. It's a maximum-capacity issue. You wouldn't understand."

Drew was surprised at how comfortable she felt around Will. Their banter didn't feel awkward or strained. It was playful and easy. As if Will was an old friend. A really adorable old friend who was still wearing the white shell necklace he made at her family's camp.

"What were the skateboarder's last words?" he asked.

"I don't know," Drew said as the melting ice she was holding to her tailbone sent trickles of water down her shorts.

"Hey, dude, watch this."

She laughed and then fired back with "How many skateboarders does it take to change a light bulb?"

He shrugged.

"Eight. One to do it and seven to post the video."

They laughed, but it was Drew who suddenly felt like the joke. Will wasn't shy. He didn't have face blindness or a personality-altering reaction to Levocetirizine. He was confident and healthy. Which meant Fonda's simple explanation was right; he didn't want to hang out. But until Drew heard him say it, she'd never fully believe it. Because there was an invisible crackle that charged the space between their bodies, and that crackle told a different story.

Why were you acting so weird at school the other day? And before you speak, know that whatever answer you give is fine as long as you're honest. Because nothing hurts more than guessing. Not even the truth, Drew wanted to say. But she didn't need to be a boy stuff expert to know that that was the opposite of Doug's advice and would not put him at ease. Instead, she asked if he wanted to skate on Saturday.

"Uh . . ." Will gazed out at the parking lot, then began opening and closing the Velcro strap on his wrist guard.

"It's okay," Drew said, rushing to fill the awkward silence. "I get it."

"It's not that," he said, still with that Velcro. "It's—"

"We can do it some other time, or never. Whatever." Drew felt a prickly rush of heat under her armpits. Did she really just rhyme?

"No, I have plans on Saturday with my friends, that's all." He looked up and met her eyes, shooting that crackle straight into her body. "But any chance you're going to the Avas' party tomorrow?"

"I wasn't invited," Drew said. "I mean, not because I'm a loser or anything. I'm new at Poplar, so I don't really know them. That's all."

"Well, you're invited now," Will said. "You can go with me. I'll introduce you."

Drew's ice pack slipped to the ground. "Actually?"

"Actually."

She felt like she was flying down the bowl again. The rush was that exhilarating. "Okay."

He stood up and then sat, his body unsure of how to react. It was adorkable.

"Want to meet at the school and ride there together?"

Despite her scrapes, bruises, and bumps, Drew had never felt more beautiful in her life.

"Sounds good."

The moment they parted ways, Drew hopped on her skateboard, feeling no pain, and pumped her foot across the pavement faster than she ever had before. She couldn't wait to share this new development with the girls, and if she was being totally honest, maybe squeak out a good-natured "I told you so" or two. Then . . . *wham!*

All of Drew's joy abruptly stopped, the way it would if she had walked into a sliding glass door. Only it wasn't glass Drew had smashed into. It was reality.

The Avas' party was tomorrow. Tomorrow was Friday. The same night as Fonda's Sleepover Spa-tacular.

Now what?

Was Drew supposed to cancel on her friends or cancel on Will? Miss the Spa-tacular or a boy-girl party with an actual boy? *The* actual boy. Should she tell her friends she'd rather be with Will or tell Will she'd rather be with her friends? No matter what Drew chose, *who* she chose, someone was going to get hurt. And that someone was probably going to be her.

chapter sixteen.

ALL WEEK LONG, every seventh grader's conversation, regardless of how it started, ended with the Avas' boy-girl party—a party Fonda was not invited to. A lifetime of being snubbed by Winfrey and Amelia was agonizing enough. Now she had to endure another year of peer snubs too? Each time someone talked about it, which was all the time, Fonda felt like her insides were being hollowed out by a cold ice cream scooper.

She tried to alleviate the pain with thoughts of the Spa-tacular and all the mud masks, playlists, sugary snacks, and Netflix that would go with it. She tried telling herself that NOT having to fuss over an outfit for the boy-girl party would be a relief. And that her own girl-girl-girl party would be way better because she could wear comfy pajamas, burp out loud, and pee with the door open. But Fonda's personal pep talks were no match for the Avas' party. Excitement was spreading through the school like lice.

Overheard in science:

Mr. Burman: *Who can use the word* blastocyst *in a sentence?*

Maya whispers to her friend Dani: *We're going to have a blast-ocyst at the Avas' party tonight.*

Overheard at lunch:

Eighth-grade girl: *How many Avas does it take to throw a party?*

Friend: *I don't know. How many?*

Eighth-grade girl: *Three.*

Friend: *I don't get it.*

Eighth-grade girl: *That wasn't a joke. It really takes three of them.*

Friend: *That means it's going to be three times as fun.*

Eighth-grade girl: *I know. I can't wait!*

Overheard in language arts:

Ms. Silver: *That's the bell. Have fun at Ava's party tonight!*

Now, in the school locker room, Fonda was tearing off her PE uniform as if it were on fire because if one more Ava said one more thing about her rhymes-with-*farty*, Fonda's hair was going to curl.

"Question," Ava H. said as she pulled a travel mirror from her backpack and began grooming her fake eyelashes with a tiny comb. "Does anyone know if Henry Goode is coming tonight?"

"It's his mom's birthday," said Ava G., her high-pitched voice echoing off the dingy white tiles. "So, I wouldn't count on it."

"Then he better not count on me having a crush on him," she told her reflection. "He's Goode but he's not that good."

They cracked up and high-fived each other while Fonda speed-tied her high-tops.

"Outfit update!" Ava G. announced.

The girls took a seat on a wooden changing bench and gave Ava G. their full attention.

"My mother said yes to the gold dress!"

Ava R. applauded. "What shoes?"

"The high school girls are doing homecoming barefoot this year. I might try it."

Ava R. turned to Fonda. "Didn't your sisters invent that?"

Fonda slammed her locker shut, pretending not to hear.

"What are you wearing?" Ava R. asked her, a little louder this time.

Fonda glanced down at her DIY pom-pom sweatshirt and leopard-print leggings. "I know, it's a bit much, but I found a glue gun last night and—"

"Whaddaya mean, bit much?" Ava H. said. "You're so Harry!"

Fonda's heart began to pound. Yes, her leg stubble *was* major at the moment. How did they know that?

"It's true," Ava G. said. "You're all Styles!"

Oh. Fonda tipped her head. "I am?"

The Avas nodded.

"What I meant was," Ava R. said, "what are you wearing *tonight*?"

"Tonight?" Fonda pictured herself in flannel pajama bottoms and a faded Meghan Trainor tank.

"Yes, tonight."

"What's tonight?"

"Very funny," Ava G. said. Then, off Fonda's confused expression, "Our party, Harry Styles."

"Your *party*?"

"Yeah. You're coming, right?"

"Um." Fonda nervously twisted her friendship bracelets. Was she missing something? "But I wasn't on that list you made."

The Avas laughed.

"That list was for guests," said Ava G. "And you're not a guest. You're practically one of us."

Fonda searched their faces for signs of insincerity— side-eye glances, mean-girl giggles, the giant "just kidding" that would inevitably burst forth from their lips. Anything that could shame Fonda for hoping that they just might, maybe, possibly, mean what they said. But all she saw were three girls nodding kindly. "Seriously?"

"You gave us period purses," said Ava R. "That's, likc, an automatic invite for life."

"You know that, right?" Ava H. said to her travel mirror as she dabbed her eyelids with glitter.

Fonda's heart stopped pounding and started to soar. She was invited. She was *invited*.

SHE WAS INVITED!

"Of course I knew that. Duh." Her cheeks burned red with shame. Λ little bit because she said *duh*, but mostly because she wasted an entire week feeling resentful and angry toward the Avas. Forget Harry Styles. Harry Hostiles had been more like it.

"So, your outfit?"

"It's a surprise," Fonda managed. Because it was, even to her. What was she going to wear? How was she going to get there? What would she say to the boys? Would there be dancing? Would anyone ask her? Did she even want them to? What about—

The run of questions in Fonda's head came to a sudden and jarring stop. *The sleepover!*

What was she going to tell the girls? How would

she tell the girls? When would she tell the girls? Would they be mad at her? Would they understand? Would they want to go with her? Could they go with her . . . ?

"Quick question," Fonda asked as the Avas gathered their bags. "Can I bring two friends?"

The Avas exchanged glances.

"They're both new here," Fonda continued. "But don't worry, I've known them my whole life and can totally vouch for them."

"I would, but my mom is being really strict about the numbers," said Ava G. with a pout. "Sorry. Maybe next time."

But next time didn't help Fonda. Because for the first time in her life, she had two separate plans for the same night—and she had no idea which one to choose.

♥

WHEN THE GIRLS got to the top of their street after school, Fonda gripped her stomach and winced. The pain was extreme. It was hot, swirling, and foreboding. Only it wasn't restricted to her stomach, like she wanted Drew and Ruthie to believe. It consumed her entire body with its soul-crushing weight, the way lies often do.

She'd spent all afternoon agonizing over what to do. She considered telling her friends the truth—that she had been invited the whole time and didn't know it. That this party was a once-in-a-lifetime opportunity and their sleepovers were weekly. That if Fonda went, it would be good for all of them, because next time she would probably get to make her own list and she'd put Drew and Ruthie at the very top.

Fonda knew that honoring plans with her nesties was the right thing to do. She also knew that she had wanted to be accepted by people like her sisters or the Avas for years. And now that she was, she couldn't just *thanks-but-no-thanks* them. This party could be the golden opportunity her fortune was referring to. And when golden opportunities knock, isn't one supposed to open the door and welcome them in?

Either way, the truth about Ruthie and Drew not being invited would come up. And Fonda knew from experience that that kind of pain hurt more than the lying kind, and she wanted to save them from that.

So, even though she *could* come clean, wasn't lying the kinder choice?

And so Fonda committed to her decision and doubled over on the sidewalk. "Owie."

"What's wrong?" Drew asked.

"Stomach," Fonda groaned. "I've had the TAG teacher all afternoon."

"Rhea?" Ruthie asked, concerned. "From what?"

"Bad chicken," Fonda said, feeling another wave of soul-crushing guilt.

All of a sudden, an ineffable look flashed over Drew's face and then she doubled over too.

"Same." Drew gripped her stomach.

"Same what?" Fonda asked.

"I ate bad chicken too."

"I thought you had salmon for lunch," Fonda said, wondering how Drew managed to catch a fake ache.

"No, it was chicken. It just looked like salmon." Drew doubled over again. "Ugh, why did I eat pink chicken?"

Ruthie's blue eyes widened with concern. "Stay here. I'll run ahead and get your moms."

Drew waved off her suggestion like a bad smell. "I think I can make it."

"Same," Fonda said, "but I might need to cancel the sleepover."

Ruthie's face went slack. "Nooo! I have a huge secret to tell you."

Fonda stopped to lean against a neighbor's mailbox for maximum effect. The metal edge dug into her back like a punishment. "Can you tell us the secret now?"

"Absolutely not," Ruthie whispered like a CIA operative. A very loud, bad one. "This secret must be delivered under the cloak of darkness."

"I agree with Fonda," Drew said as she shuffled weakly down the block. "I think we should cancel."

Ruthie frowned. "But we've never canceled a sleepover."

"We've never both had food poisoning," Drew pointed out.

"I have an idea!" Fonda said. "Why don't we move it to tomorrow?"

It was the perfect solution. How had she not thought of it sooner? She would go to the party, Drew could recover from her real food poisoning, and they'd have the Spa-tacular twenty-four hours later.

"We can't have a Friday-night sleepover on a Saturday," Ruthie insisted.

"Who cares what day it is, as long as we're together?" Fonda said, faking another cramp. "Uh-oh, I think I've got Ruthie's teacher! Gotta go."

With that, she made a run for home and didn't look back. Anything to get away from the disappointment on Ruthie's face. Disappointment *she* caused. But she would make it up to them the very next day by throwing a spectacular Saturday Spa-tacular. In the meantime, she was going to find out how popular girls did parties, boys, and life—and make sure she, Drew, and Ruthie got on every invite list for the rest of the year. Once she did, her lies wouldn't matter.

The nesties would.

chapter seventeen.

"HOMEWORK ON A Friday night?" said Steven, Ruthie's father, as he entered her bedroom. Her mother followed, along with the spicy cherry scent of her perfume. He was wearing a tuxedo. She, a navy satin dress. They looked like actual people, not parents.

Ruthie shut her laptop and turned to face them with a fake I'm-totally-at-peace-with-my-situation grin, which was the real homework. Because on the inside, she was bummed to the power of ten knowing her best friends were too sick to hang out. She was, however, grateful that Rhea was teaching her how to write a novel. The characters Ruthie created for her "Foxie the Werefox" story were much-needed companions.

"Is it too intense?" Fran asked, worried.

"A little," Ruthie said. She didn't like when her mother wore too much perfume. It gave her a headache. "Maybe just one spritz instead of two next time."

"No." Fran laughed. "I was talking about TAG. We want you to feel challenged, not overwhelmed." She sat on the corner of Ruthie's desk and crossed her legs. "Remember the conversation we had about Foxie— whether she should follow her head or her heart? Could that have also been about you? It seemed like she was struggling with the same kinds of issues as you."

"How is that even possible? I'm not a lycanthrope," Ruthie said, trying to deflect. Yes, she knew lycanthropes were wolves and that Foxie was a fox. But her mother didn't, and that word was almost as fun as *oodles*, so she said it anyway.

"Fair enough." Fran exhaled sharply. "Bad analogy. The point is, your father and I have been wondering if the TAG workload is too . . . intense."

"Why would you say that?" Ruthie asked, not sure if she should be relieved or offended.

"Well, you just seem so down lately. Are you overwhelmed?"

Ruthie glimpsed at the puzzles on her walls, the

books and board games on her shelves, the spelling bee trophies . . . all proof that her brain needed TAG. But her mom did say the heart mattered more, so in keeping with her plan, she said, "It's hard, but I'm doing my best."

"Your best is all we can ask for." Steven kissed her forehead. "Proud of you."

We'll see how proud you are on Monday when I get my test results back, Ruthie thought as her insides roiled with guilt. She hated lying to her parents, hated pretending she couldn't keep up with the Titans, and hated knowing that her friends—the only ones who would be truly happy about all of this—were sick and there was nothing she could do to help. The whole situation made Ruthie feel like she ate bad chicken too.

"We should get going," Steven told Fran.

"I just don't like that she's home alone on a Friday night," Fran said, as if Ruthie wasn't there.

"I can't help it. My sleepover was canceled."

"Isn't there someone from TAG you can hang out with?" Fran asked. "We could drop you off on our way to dinner and pick you up on our way home."

Ruthie considered this, but only for a moment. It would feel weird hanging out with someone new on a

Friday night. As awkward and clunky as writing with her left hand. Especially since Drew and Fonda were sick. "Everyone has plans."

"Everyone?" Fran pressed.

Ruthie opened her mouth to answer, then remembered Sage's invitation to hang out. The idea of accepting did trigger that left-handed awkward feeling, but Sage *had* asked.

"There is one person," Ruthie said as she flipped open her laptop and began typing an email.

> **RUTHIE:** Are you still around tonight?
>
> **SAGE:** Affirmative. My stepsister is throwing a party at our house. Want to come? We can spy on the dumb-dumbs.
>
> **RUTHIE:** Affirmative. My parents will drop me soon.
>
> **SAGE:** Wear all black. It's better for spying. Hurry!

With a renewed sense of hope, Ruthie opened her closet, rummaged past her happy patterns and adorable kitten tees, in search of the only black items she owned: leggings with black fringe up the sides left over from her short-lived modern dance phase and a matching leotard. Footwear, however, was proving to be a problem. She grabbed a pair of polka-dot sneakers, figuring she could kick them off when she got to Sage's. Going barefoot would be better for sneaking around anyway.

"Interesting look," Fran said when Ruthie got into the car.

"Oh, to be young again." Steven laughed as he backed out of the driveway.

Ruthie waved a sad goodbye to Drew's and Fonda's houses as they drove up the street. Spending Friday night with someone new felt a lot like cheating. But she'd bring them ginger ale in the morning and tell them about her night in such vivid detail, they'd think they were there.

chapter eighteen.

"IF YOU'RE NOT having fun, just call me," Drew's father said as he pulled into the school parking lot. "Mom or I can come get you anytime."

Drew leaned over and kissed him on the cheek, which wasn't exactly an easy thing to do in a helmet and skate pads. "Don't worry, Daddy. It'll be fine."

But would it? What were she and Will supposed to talk about all night? *The Skateboard Kid*? Then what? Camp? Classes? Teachers? *Borrrr-ing*. If only she could ask her friends.

As her father pulled away, Drew began to regret her bad chicken claim. Lying to the girls felt sinister, but also a little tragic. She would have preferred it if the scene played out something like:

Guess what? Will asked me to go to that party! And they'd be all, *No way! Let's help you pick out a comfortable yet flattering outfit.* And she'd be all, *What about the Spatacular?* And they'd be all, *We can do that tomorrow night. This is an epic opportunity to get to know your crush. You have to go.* And she'd be all, *You guys are the most supportive friends ever.* And they'd be all, *So are you.* Then they'd hug and make Drew promise to send pics.

But the conversation would never go like that. Instead, Fonda would think less of Drew for even considering it. She'd say things like *Will doesn't deserve you,* and *You're choosing an emotionally immature doozer with face blindness over us?* and Ruthie would say, *What? I can't hear you. I'm wearing invisible noise-canceling headphones!* Mostly because she hated conflict, but also because she didn't have any devices, so real headphones would be useless.

So, when Fonda said she was sick, Drew thought it would be easier to say the same. The sleepover was canceled anyway, so what harm could come of it?

Actually, Drew, a ton of harm can come from it, she thought as she skated toward their meeting spot. She had to admit that despite her five reasons, her friends had a point. She had never even hung out with Will, and yet he managed to bum her out. What if he treated her like a stranger all over again? Or worse? What if he didn't show? Then what? It wasn't like she could run crying to Fonda and Ruthie about it. They thought she was at home with Ruthie's teacher!

Drew considered turning around, claiming miraculous recovery, and bringing Fonda ginger ale and toast when a boy dressed in skinny jeans, a turquoise tee, and red sneaks came skating toward her, his smile so sparkly she giggled like a girl with nothing to say. It was too much for one person to handle.

"Hey," Will said as he approached.

"My parents made me wear these," Drew responded, indicating her body armor.

"Good idea."

"What's that supposed to mean?" Drew giggled (again).

"I saw you skate. That's all."

"That wipeout was your fault!"

"My fault?" He kicked up his board and caught it. "How?"

"Don't get me stah-ted."

She laughed a little longer than the joke deserved to avoid an uncomfortable silence. Then Will suggested they get going.

"I thought you'd never ask," Drew answered in some strange Harry Potter–type accent that she instantly regretted. Did every girl feel like a malfunctioning robot when she was alone with someone she liked?

They headed down Temple Road—a winding neighborhood street that allowed for long, lazy swerves. As they skated, the sun began to sink behind the ocean, its final kiss of light landing on their faces like a blessing. If Drew had been watching this scene in a movie, she would have envied the girl for living inside such a perfect moment. But Drew *was* that girl. And the moment, the boy, the sunset, the winding road . . . they were all hers.

She wanted to ask Will if he liked the sound of wheels grinding on asphalt, if that was his favorite song too? But unlike the girl in her imaginary movie, this scene didn't come with a script. What if he thought she was bananas?

It was funny. Drew had had hundreds of imaginary

conversations with Will in her head, but now that they were on an official skate hang, she had no clue what to say. There were so many little things she wanted to know, like what he watched on TV, what he liked to snack on, and were his parents embarrassing too? If so, how embarrassing? Because they couldn't possibly be more embarrassing than hers. But there was one big question that took priority over all the little ones. The little ones would have to wait.

"So, I have a question," Drew said, pulling up beside Will. Now, she didn't have to be a boy stuff expert to know that asking a guy why he'd been weird was a major no-no. That she was supposed to act aloof and unaffected by his moodiness because, well, her mother's bathroom magazines said so. But, really? Who got answers by not asking? "Remember when I saw you on the first day of school?"

"Uh, yeah."

"Oh, good. I can cross amnesia off the list," she said, wishing Fonda and Ruthie were there to appreciate her snark.

"Huh?"

"You acted like you didn't know me."

"Yeah." Will lowered his head. "About that . . ."

Drew's mouth went dry. She knew it. There *was* a reason. And judging by his guilty expression, shyness was not it. This reason had an element of secrecy to it, maybe conspiracy. Even his white shell necklace seemed to be in on it. The way it wrapped itself around him like a protective sidekick, ready to defend him at all costs. But Drew was not going to be intimidated. She was determined to get an explanation, no matter how unpleasant it was. "Then why were you—"

"What up, Wilbur?" called a blond boy as he stepped out of a Prius. An even blonder blond got out next. They were both wearing surf trunks instead of shorts.

"What up?" Will said back with a sharp wave that seemed to say, *Just because we know each other doesn't mean we're friends.* Then, quietly to Drew, "That's Dune Wolsey. He's been calling me Wilbur ever since we read *Charlotte's Web* in third grade. Five more years, and I'll never have to hear that again."

"Unless you go to the same college," Drew said, defeated. The moment, *their* moment, was gone.

"True." He smirked and then slowed his pace. Was

he intentionally putting some distance between himself and the boys, or was Will getting cold feet about showing up with Drew? "Dope house, right?" he said, drawing her out of her head.

"Yeah," she managed, because confusion aside, Ava G.'s house *was* dope. It was made of concrete and glass and had a front garden filled with cacti that resembled outlaws in the fading light. Green rocking chairs flanked the colossal wood door like emerald earrings, and the mailbox was an exact replica of the home.

"Museum goals," Drew said, temporarily forgetting all about his *about that . . .* comment. Because she was about to walk into a party with Will Wilder, and how stressful and awesome was that? (Or "strawsome," as her mother would say.)

Ava G. threw open the door before they had a chance to ring the bell. Her hair was piled into a thick bun on top of her head and sprayed gold to match her dress. She looked like an Oscar.

"Wilder!" she said in a high-pitched squeal. Without another word, she pinch-gripped their skateboards and tossed them outside like dead animals. "Hi, I'm Ava," she told Drew, lips teetering between a smile and a frown.

"Drew. I'm new."

"Wilder, is she with you?"

"Yep."

Ava G. flicked a glance at Drew's outfit—jeans, Vans, white T-shirt. Compared to her, Drew looked like the other Oscar, the one that's green, grouchy, and lives in a trash can. "Are you going to keep those on?" she asked, pointing at her pads. "I can hide them in my room if you want."

"Uh—"

"Yes," Will said dryly. "Yes, she is."

Drew giggled. *Challenge accepted.*

"Welll-come!" bellowed a mom, who moved toward them with the tight quick steps of a runner who couldn't be bothered to stretch. "Did Ava tell you?" she said, thrusting a basket toward them. "This is a no-phone zone."

They dropped their phones inside and were told to make themselves comfortable. Which was easier said than done. Despite the sea-glass-colored walls, driftwood picture frames, and ceramic starfish, nothing about the house was comfortable. The lights were bright, the music was classical, and the all-white furniture was protected by towels. Girls sat stiffly on the couch while boys stood in a cluster by the bookshelves. This wasn't a party. It was a library. And the worst part was Drew couldn't tell Fonda about any of it. She couldn't say *You'd have cooler music* or *You'd have better snacks* or *You're more fun than all the Avas put together*, because Fonda could never know Drew was there. Could never know she chose Will over the Spa-tacular. Could never know she was leaving her skate pads on because Will thought it was hilarious. The whole thing felt like a giant punishment for lying. One Drew knew she deserved, but she resented nonetheless.

"So, back to my other question," she said, stopping Will before they braved the living room. She was aware of the eyes watching them. Eyes that wanted to know what the adorable seventh-grade boy was doing with the new girl and why she was dressed like a stormtrooper. But Drew decided that standing close to the front door was more important than mingling, in case his answer made her cry and she needed to bolt.

As if also sensing the eyes, Will took Drew by the

hand, led her through the kitchen and out the sliding glass doors onto the porch. His touch sent electrical currents throughout her entire body. Maybe she *was* a lamp.

"What is it?" Drew pressed. "You're freaking me out."

Will leaned against the glass railing, took a deep breath, and exhaled. "Henry Goode likes you."

"Who?"

"The guy I was skating with at lunch that day. He thought you were, you know, cool, I guess."

"What are you talking about?"

"Henry. He's in your PE class."

"And?"

"At the beginning of lunch that first day, he said there was a cute new girl named Drew and he wanted to hang out with you."

"And?"

"He called dibs."

Drew could feel her heart beating against her scalp. "Dibs?"

"Like, he saw you first."

"So what?"

"So you're off-limits."

"Ew!" Drew said. "For one, he didn't see me first; you did. For two, I get to decide when I'm off-limits. And for three, I'm a person, not the last slice of pizza. He can't claim me."

"I know," Will said. "That's what I told him, but without the pizza part."

Was this good news or bad news? Was Will being respectful or ridiculous? Should she be flattered or furious? Drew looked out at the backyard, giving her tangled thoughts a moment to sort themselves out.

"The trees look like broccoli, don'cha think?" Will said.

It was the kind of comment Drew would have appreciated under different circumstances. But now? It seemed like he was trying to change the subject. "I don't get it."

Will pointed at the treetops. "I know it's dark, but if you look closely—"

"Not the broccoli thing. The Henry thing."

Will ran a hand through his hair. "When I told Henry he couldn't call dibs, he asked if I liked you. I didn't want to start a whole thing, so I panicked and—"

Everything inside Drew sped up. *He said the L-word! He said the L-word! He said the L-word! He said the L-word! He said the L-word! He said the L-word! He said the L-word! He said the L-word!* "And *what?*"

"I said I didn't know who you were."

"Well, do you?"

"Yeah, doofus, we met at Battleflag, remember?"

This time Drew couldn't help but smile. "No, I meant do you *like me?*"

Was it bold? Very. But she couldn't waste another millisecond of her life guessing and assessing. The truth had been waiting outside long enough. It was time to let it in.

When Will opened his mouth to answer, Drew almost yelled, *STOP!* She wanted to freeze time, crawl inside the sliver of space between knowing and not knowing as if it were a sleeping bag, and zip it all the way to the top. Keep the truth outside a little longer and stay in that place where everything she wanted was still possible.

"Do I what?" Will asked, with a devilish half smile.

"Do you like me?"

"I dunno." Will glanced out at the broccoli. Then down at his sneakers. "Do you like *me?*"

"That depends."

He met her eyes. "On what?"

"Are you going to act like you don't know me when Henry's around?"

"That depends too."

"On what?"

"Are you going to wear those pads to school on Monday?"

Drew laughed. "Probably."

"Then I will definitely act like I know you."

"Even if Henry's around?"

Will smiled. "Especially if Henry's around." He looked down at his toes and kicked a few pebbles before catching her eye again. "Look, I'm sorry I ignored you. That wasn't cool. Do-over?"

"Do-over." Drew smiled back. She couldn't wait to tell her friends! But *ugh*—she was supposed to be puking chicken, not having the best conversation of all time. Now, instead of celebrating, she'd have to keep the broccoli trees, her bravery, the L-word, and Will's emotional maturity from them forever. Which almost made the night seem pointless.

Almost.

chapter nineteen.

REGRET WRAPPED ITSELF around Fonda like a stinky hug and squeezed. She faked bad chicken, lied to her best friends, and spent forty minutes curating the perfect outfit for *this*? The lights were doctor's-office bright; the music was elevator-y. And were those baby carrots in the snack bowl? It reminded Fonda of a toddler birthday party, except boys and girls talked to each other at those.

She considered calling Drew to see how she was feeling, but contact with the outside world was no longer an option. Ava G.'s mother had taken her phone.

"Styles!" Ava H. called from the towel-covered couch. If her metallic leggings weren't enough to get Fonda's attention, her black sequin top certainly was. "Get over here!"

Chin lifted and chest thrust, Fonda catwalked into the living room wearing what she hoped would establish her as an out-of-the-box thinker. Silk kimono, black shorts, and wedge sandals. It was attractive, not try-hard. Fashionable, not trendy.

"Love the look!" Ava G. said, snapping a picture with her invisible phone.

"Yours too," Fonda managed, even though Ava G. was twinning with an Academy Award.

"I want," said Ava R. "How can I shop it?"

Have a birthday party at Ginger Sushi. The kimono is free with a group of seven or more, Fonda didn't dare admit. Instead, she just said, "It's vintage."

"Really?" Ava R. said. "That's super ann."

"Who's Super Ann?" Fonda asked.

"Super ann-oying." She pouted. "Now I can't get it."

"I can take you shopping," Fonda offered. "I know a bunch of great vintage shops."

"Super yay!" Ava R. said.

"What does that stand for?"

"Just a lot of yay."

Fonda laughed. And not in that phony I'm-trying-to-fit-in sort of way. She was genuinely amused. All those years she spent resenting the Avas for not "seeing" her suddenly seemed childish and unnecessary. A total waste of what could have been fun. Because as it happened, all she had to do was step out of the shadows and show them she was there. Sure, it took a generous scoop of courage and a dash of effort, but once she did it, everything changed. So much so that Fonda was starting to wonder if she was wrong to want her own friend group. Maybe the power move was to merge: bring in her girls, become one *giant* group, and dominate that way. Like the game Infection, where one person starts off as It and, when they tag someone, that new person becomes It too. The more people they tag, the more Its there are. Soon the minority becomes the majority, the little becomes the big.

"Speaking of muses," Ava H. said, "who do you think's gonna land the PP?"

"Easy. The blonde in the knee pads," said Ava G. "I mean, who wears that to a party?"

Fonda smiled to herself. Drew would. Then, "What's a PP?"

"I think it'll be Jasper and Frankie," said Ava H., ignoring Fonda's question. "I heard they were going to cut the power."

Ava G. side-eyed the clump of boys by the bookshelves. "They better not, or my stepdad will sue."

"What's a PP?" Fonda asked again.

"Anyway, how are we going to get a PP in the dark?" Ava R. asked.

"Will someone please tell me—"

"It stands for party post," Ava R. explained. "It's the VOTN that goes viral."

"VOTN?"

"Video of the night. Someone always does something embarrassing, and we always record it."

"But we don't have our phones," Fonda said. Aware that she said "we" and double aware that no one corrected her and said, *You're not a we. You're a you. Only we're we's.*

"My parents are only staying for ten more minutes," Ava G. whispered, then lifted an eyebrow as if to say, *Know what I mean?*

Fonda did not.

"Every party, they say they're going to stay until the end, but they always get bored early. You can tell my mom's about to lose it when she starts rubbing her forehead. See?"

Sure enough, Ava's mom was watching the crowd of kids with a deepening frown. She let out a sigh and rubbed her temples dramatically. And as Ava G. predicted, exactly ten minutes later, her mom and stepdad went to the guesthouse to watch a movie.

The moment they were gone, Ava G. called, "Showtime!" and everyone sprang into action. Boys began pushing couches against the walls, girls unloaded sodas and chips from their backpacks, Ava R. changed the music, and Ava H. dimmed the lights. Before long, crushes were flirting freely, and the Avas got everyone dancing to the electronic beats of "Mi Rumba." They had clearly done this before. Many times.

"Come awn, Styles!" shouted Ava R. as she yanked Fonda into the center of their undulating mass. All around her bodies were jumping, sweating, twirling. Hands were waving, fists were pumping, and baby carrots were getting tossed like confetti.

When the song changed to GRiZ's "I'm Good," Fonda kicked off her shoes, not caring if anyone thought she was copying her sisters, and sang, "Na na na na na na na na na," with everyone else.

Until that moment, Fonda had no idea it was possible to have fun without Drew and Ruthie. She missed them, she really did, and wished they had been invited. Then they'd be all sweaty and out of breath from doing the Nae Nae too. They'd be singing their throats raw and freestyle dancing with kids who weren't so bad after all. And they'd finally understand why Fonda was trying so hard. Maybe they'd even start trying hard too.

But as she danced, all thoughts of her friends and nestie domination fell away. There was something so relaxing about *being* in the good time instead of trying to *create* it. About not having to worry about anyone's fun but her own. And Fonda was determined to enjoy every sweaty second.

chapter twenty.

SAGE AND RUTHIE settled between the succulent garden and the living room window of Sage's house, then
froze to make sure they hadn't been detected.

"I can't believe you and Ava G. live together," Ruthie
whispered as she lowered her EyeClops Infrared Stealth
Goggles. She looked like a fly with her wide plastic eyes,
black tights, and leotard. Meanwhile, Sage, who always
wore black, looked exactly like herself. Except for the
gold high-tops, which had been replaced by black ballet
slippers.

"I know. It was super weird at first, but it's been
about a year, so . . ."

Deciding the coast was clear, they rose up and began spying on the dance party.

"How did that even happen?" Ruthie asked, her eyes fixed on Ava G.

"Gold hair spray and a lot of nerve."

"No." Ruthie smiled. "The two of you living together."

"Well, Ruthie," Sage began, "when a man and woman love each other . . ."

"No, really." Ruthie laughed, suddenly aware that she was spending Friday night with someone new. And not hating it at all. "What's the story?"

"My mom died when I was two, my dad and Ava's mom started dating when I was nine, they got married when I was eleven, and Ava and I stopped ignoring each other last month. She's a dumb-dumb, but my dad says I need to try."

Ruthie felt a rush of prickly tingles all over her body. Would Sage think *she* was a dumb-dumb when she left TAG? "Why do you call everyone that?"

Sage pointed past the window, at the bouncing throng inside. "Look at them. What about any of that seems intelligent to you?"

"It's not supposed to be intelligent," Ruthie said. "It's supposed to be fun."

"Please," Sage said, adjusting her glasses. "They're doing it because they don't have anything to say. I mean, dancing is so weird, am I right?" Then in her best caveman voice she added, "Uh, let's bang on instruments and flail around."

Sage did have a point. Dancing *was* ridiculous if you really thought about it. "It's like kissing," Ruthie said, doing her best caveman. "Uh, let's press our lips together and make *mmmmm* noises."

"What about clapping? Let's all smack our hands together to show how much we like you."

"Or breathing," Ruthie said. Then she took it back. "No one really invented that, did they?"

"Hey," Sage said, her attention back on the party. "Isn't that your friend?"

"My friend?" Ruthie asked, trying to generate a list of possibilities. She couldn't come up with a single name. Both of her friends were sick at home. "Who?"

"The one you walk home with after school."

Ruthie adjusted the focus on her lenses, pressed her face up to the window, and bristled. There was a girl inside who looked exactly like Fonda, and she was doing the Nae Nae with the Avas. Her hair was flat-ironed, her feet were bare, and she was trying to pass a Ginger Sushi bathrobe off as outerwear. Ruthie lifted her goggles and drew back her head, her heart beating erratically in her chest. "How is this even possible?"

Sage sighed. "Anything's possible with dumb-dumbs."

Ruthie stood. Her body wanted to spring into action, but her brain was still trying to catch up. Was there really a Fonda look-alike running around town? Assuming there was, and she also went to Poplar Middle, and also had a bathrobe from Ginger Sushi, wouldn't they have heard about her? Or was that dancing girl the real Fonda? Real, but *fake*.

"I have eyes on a possible double agent," Ruthie said, trying to stay in character. Because the moment she stopped playing spy and started playing herself, she'd have to accept that one of her best friends lied about being sick so she could go to a party without her, and that was too much hurt to handle all at once.

"We have to infiltrate. She needs to be questioned."

"We'll be exposed!" Ruthie said, hands shaking.

"That's a chance I'm willing to take." Sage pulled Ruthie up to stand. "Let's move."

The moment they reached the front door, the lights went out, the music stopped, and everyone began to scream.

"What's happening?" Ruthie asked.

"I'm not sure," Sage said, "but we've just been granted cover." She focused her night vision goggles and led the way. "Follow me."

chapter twenty-one.

A SWELL OF razor-edged screams popped Drew's crush bubble and sent her crashing down to reality. "What's going on in there?" she asked as Will pressed his face against the sliding glass doors to investigate.

"I can't see," he said. "It's horror-movie dark in there." Then he snickered. "I can't believe they went through with it."

"Who went through with what?"

"Jasper and Frankie. They've been planning all week to cut the power."

Drew had zero idea how one would cut the power, and she was in no mood to figure it out. Will L-worded her. She L-worded him. The only thing she was in the mood to do was attack life. Because L-wording someone who L-worded you back was a full-body rush that had the ability to transform unappealing situations into exciting adventures. Even mass hysteria.

"Come on," she urged. "Let's check it out."

"I thought you'd never ask," he answered, with his own strange Harry Potter–type accent.

"What's going on in there?" called Ava's stepdad as he and his wife hurried from the guesthouse.

"Are we being robbed?" panted Ava's mother.

"What kind of robber would break into a house full of teenagers?" he said, wiping his sweaty brow. "Teenagers are nature's burglar alarms. Even the most hardened criminals are afraid of them."

"Well, how do you explain—"

"I think some guys in our grade pulled a prank," Will said, making direct eye contact with the grown-ups. Drew thought about her parents and how they would have liked that.

Then came a sudden crash of glass.

"My mirror!" Ava's mother screamed.

Her stepfather whispered, "Never again," under his breath and then they charged inside.

"I gotta see this!" Will took Drew by the hand and

led her into the dark kitchen. His touch sent enough electricity through her to light not just the house but the entire block.

How was she supposed to keep all these moments from Fonda and Ruthie? It was wrong to let them think Will was standoffish, rude, and unworthy of her affection, especially since he was the opposite. But what about this was *right*? Admitting she faked food poisoning so she could sneak off to a party? They'd never talk to her again.

Down the hall, kids were screaming, knocking into walls, and urging one another to find the basket of phones.

"Oof," Drew said as her hip collided with the edge of the dining table. The kitchen was outer-space dark.

"Told ya you needed those pads," Will teased.

Then came the sound of footsteps. "Someone's coming," Drew whispered.

"Duck!"

They crouched down behind the kitchen island and cupped hands over mouths to contain their giggles.

"I call time-out on the mission so I can grab some chips," said a girl as she entered the kitchen. "I think better while I'm chewing."

"Fine, but hurry," another girl whispered back.

"I am a ghossst," Will bellowed from their hiding spot.

Drew began to quake with laughter.

"Who's there?" asked the chips girl.

"Alec," Will said.

"Alec *who*?"

"Alec-tricity is out!"

Drew snorted a little.

"Yeah, I kinda figured that. Now, seriously, who are you?"

"It's Avery," Will said.

"Avery? Avery who?"

"Avery one of you is in dangerrrrrrrrr."

Drew laughed so hard she smacked Will on the back. The sound of which made them laugh even harder.

"Um, note to dumb-dumb. This is my kitchen. So if anyone's in danger, it's you. Now, stop cowering and show yourself."

"Who cares about the ghost?" said her friend. "We need to stay focused on the mission."

There was a familiar wobbly quality to her voice. Which was odd, because the only person who spoke with that wobble was—

Ruthie.

Drew stopped laughing. *I have to get out of here!* she wanted to tell Will. But Drew couldn't speak. She couldn't breathe. She couldn't stop breathing. What was Ruthie doing at the Avas' party? The only move was to stay low, get to that sliding glass door, and sneak outside.

Without a word to Will, Drew began crawling. The plastic from her pads clicked against the hardwood floors. She sounded like a scuttling cockroach or a dog in need of a toenail clipping.

"What's that?" asked Ruthie.

Drew froze.

"I don't hear anything," said her mysterious companion. Someone reached inside the chip bag. While they crunched, Drew took off again.

"Hear that?" Ruthie said, moving closer. "Fall in!"

The bag of chips was tossed onto the counter. "Do you need backup?"

"Roger that," said Ruthie, who, for some reason, was talking like a Navy SEAL.

Then came the swoosh of stockinged feet sliding across the floor. Drew remembered how she, Ruthie, and Fonda used to wear their slipperiest socks and pretend to figure skate down her hallway. Only these feet weren't light and graceful. They were determined and—

"Drew?" said Ruthie. She was standing above her now, wearing some contraption over her eyes that must have helped her see in the dark. "What are you doing here?" Her voice was soft and mealy. Her expression shocked and confused.

Drew was stunned into silence. What could she possibly say that would make this all right? If only she could float away like a real ghost and disappear forever. Anything to avoid facing what she had done. Because as soon as Ruthie realized that Drew had gone behind her back and chosen Will over her, the relaxed wobble in her voice would harden into anger, and her confusion would calcify into contempt, and Drew did not want to be responsible for that. Because Ruthie was joy and pineapple pajamas. Not anger and contempt.

Still, of all the things Drew could have said in that moment, the only thing she could manage was "When did you get night vision goggles?"

And that didn't help one single bit.

chapter twenty-two.

THE LIGHTS POPPED on at the party, and the boiling hysteria instantly cooled.

Girls began wiping streaks of mascara from their damp eyes, then smiled as if they'd never been better. Boys fanned their sweaty armpits and teased each other for panicking.

"Found the basket!" someone shouted from the kitchen. A stampede of thirty-plus guests charged down the hallway to reclaim their phones.

Minutes later, Fonda was tapping on her screen, certain she'd find a few *How are you feeling?* texts from her friends. There were none. Which was fine. Ruthie was probably trying to give her space so she could rest, and Drew *actually* ate bad chicken, so—

"What the heck?" screeched a familiar voice.

Fonda looked up from her screen and clutched the kitchen island to keep herself from collapsing. "Ruthie?" Her mouth went dry. All distant sounds of chatter fell away.

"Fonda?" asked another familiar voice. It was Drew this time. She was on the opposite side of the island wearing knee pads and wrist guards.

Heat bloomed inside Fonda's body. Blood pounded against her scalp . . . her teeth . . . her spine. Was this a fever dream? Some kind of psychotic break? A guilt hallucination? Fonda blinked twice, hoping to erase them, but they were still there. Glaring and infuriated.

She wanted to apologize. Explain her side. Beg for mercy. Cry. Time travel. Run! But her brain was so jumbled. "What are you doing here?" spilled out before she could do any of that.

Ruthie smacked her hands down on the marble countertop and said, "I'll ask the questions!" She was positioned at the head of the island between Fonda and Drew, night vision goggles resting atop her head, blue eyes wide and damp. "Bad chicken, huh?"

"Ruthie, I'm so—"

"Food poisoning, huh?"

"I can expl—"

"You lied! You said you had my teacher!"

"Wait," Drew said to Fonda. "You lied about that?"

"Did you?" Fonda demanded.

The Avas, along with dozens of other kids, were standing around the island, cell phones aimed at the girls. How long had they been there?

"Can we go outside and talk about this?" Fonda muttered, indicating the crowd of spectators. She needed to know what Ruthie and Drew were doing there; she needed to make things right. But not in front of the Poplar paparazzi.

"Canwegooutsideandtalkaboutthis?" Ruthie mocked. "So what if everyone is watching? Is that all you care about?"

"Is *what* all I care about?"

"What people think of us?"

"Us?" Fonda scoffed. "There hasn't been an *us* since you joined TAG."

"At least the TAG'ers aren't liars, conspirators, and backstabbers."

Sage pumped her fist toward the ceiling. "Go, Titans!"

"We did *not* conspire," Drew clarified. "I had no idea Fonda was going to be here." Then to Fonda, "Why didn't you tell me?"

"Why didn't you tell *me*?"

Drew lowered her eyes. "You would have called me pathetic."

"What?" Fonda asked, feeling supremely ganged up on. And a little confused. How did Drew get invited? How did Ruthie? And how could Drew say that? "Why would I do that?"

Drew flicked her head toward Will, who was standing by the sliding glass door. The cell phones pivoted left, a school of fish changing course.

"Wait," Ruthie said. "You lied so you could come here with *him*? The doozer you said you wouldn't cross the road to help, *even* if he was injured?"

"Drew, you said *that*?" Will asked, with a mouth full of chips.

"No!"

"Yes, she did," Jasper said. "I heard her say it in the movie theater."

"Movie theater?" Will asked, looking between Drew and Jasper. "When did you two go to a movie together?"

"We didn't," Drew said just as Jasper said, "Last Saturday."

"Wait." Drew turned to Ruthie. "How do *you* know I said that? You weren't even there."

"Fonda told me."

"Thanks a lot, Fonda."

"I—" This fight was going from bad to worse, and Fonda had no clue how to stop it.

"So, Drew, you *did* say that?" Will asked.

"Yes. I mean no. I mean I said it, but I didn't—"

"Diss!" shouted Frankie.

"Major diss," said Jasper.

"Poor Wilbur," said Dune Wolsey. "I think he showed up with her." Then he paused and added, "Unless that was Jasper."

Soon everyone was chanting diss, and before Drew could stop him, Will opened the sliding glass door and took off.

"Can we *please* talk about this outside?" Fonda asked, desperate to escape the spotlight she had so often craved.

"Why?" Ruthie's eyes were wild with emotion. "You don't want these dumb-dumbs to know we're friends? Are you *that* embarrassed by me?"

Fonda felt like she had been kicked in the stomach. *Dumb-dumbs?* Was that seriously what Ruthie thought of everyone who wasn't in TAG? Was that what she thought of Drew and Fonda? "Only because you used the word *dumb-dumbs*," she lied.

Everyone laughed, and Fonda instantly regretted it. But *dumb-dumbs*? Really? Who thought that? Who *said* that? "Can we please just go somewhere private and talk about it? I'm sure we all have good reasons for—"

"For what?" Ruthie asked, her shock morphing into anger. "Lying? Betraying each other? Social climbing? Forget talking. We have nothing to talk about." She made a fist with her right hand, quickly knocked *done* onto the island in Morse code, then opened the sliding glass door to leave. When she did, her friendship bracelets got caught on the handle, their strings ripped, and hundreds of beads scattered across the floor. "You two just put the *end* in *friend*," she said, her eyes full of tears. Then she slipped into the darkness with Sage following closely behind.

"Is everyone okay?" asked Ava G.'s mother, panic etched into her face as she came running into the room.

"We're more than okay," whispered Ava R. to Fonda. "We just got our PP."

Fonda wanted to swat Ava's phone to the floor, as if that could possibly erase what had to have been the most mortifying experience of her life. Even if that did destroy Ava's video, it wouldn't matter. There were dozens more just like it. Each one a digital reminder to be careful what you wish for. Especially if that wish is to be Poplar Middle School's most-watched girl on social media ever.

chapter twenty-three.

THE TITANS WERE lazing under the pagoda during the last period on Monday—a "Monday Moment," as Rhea called it. She sold the break as an opportunity for everyone to reconnect after the weekend, but it was really a chance for her to finish grading their Thursday tests. And Ruthie was relishing the afternoon gossip session with the Titans, especially now that she was officially best-friendless.

"You really said, 'You put the *end* in *friend*'?" Alberta asked, for the fifth time.

Ruthie raised her palm. "Guilty as charged."

Alberta lay back on the pile of Moroccan cushions, as if she had just finished a satisfying meal. "Genius."

"It really was," said Sage, clearly proud to have been an eyewitness. "The dumb-dumbs were dumb-struck when she busted them."

Favian opened his mouth and pointed at the glistening puddle under his tongue. "Look, I'm lit-er-ally salivating from the drama of it all. I swear, this story has a Pavlovian hold on me."

"I wish I'd seen it," said Tomoyo.

"You *can* see it." Ruthie beamed. "It's viral!"

That she could say that with such positivity, such pride, was not lost on her. Less than twenty hours ago, Ruthie was curled up on her bed, sobbing and snotting all over Foxie. She couldn't eat, she couldn't sleep, she couldn't write. How could her so-called friends lie and ditch her like that?

Sage kept calling Drew and Fonda dumb-dumbs, but Ruthie was the one who felt like a dumb-dumb. This was exactly what Ruthie had been worried about since Fonda pointed out those TAG letters on her schedule the first day of school. Drew and Fonda had moved on without her, and Ruthie was too naïve, too much of a dumb-dumb to see it coming.

Had her brain not craved something to chew on—something other than betrayal—Ruthie would have claimed bad chicken and spent the day in bed. But she was done dwelling on the girls who stabbed her in the back. The Titans had her back now and would help it heal. Yes, she lost two friends, but she gained eight.

"I have a question," said Zandra. "You told the dark-haired one, and I quote, 'You said you had my teacher.' Were you referring to Rhea, and if so, what exactly does that mean?"

Thankfully, the ancient sound bowls rang before she could answer. The day was over. All they had to do now was get their grades and—

Ruthie stopped short of the entrance, her body weighted with regret. What had she done? She was going to get the F-word on her tests. And failing meant taking regular classes, where her brain would starve and her heart would get thrashed by Drew and Fonda yet again.

The only thing for Ruthie to do was stay after class and confess. But how could she ever explain? How could she tell Rhea that she'd thrown her grades to be with friends who didn't even care about her?

But Rhea didn't end up returning the tests. Instead

she told everyone to have a great night and asked Ruthie to stay after class.

"Funny you should ask that," Ruthie said, approaching her teacher's desk. "Because there's something I wanted to talk to you about."

"Great," Rhea said with a distracted smile. "Your mother and father should be here any moment. We can talk about it together."

"My mother and fa—"

Then, "Hello, Ruth-Ann," Steven said as they entered the room.

The Goldmans were dressed in their work clothes—Fran in pink scrubs and Steven in a suit—which meant they rushed over from work three hours before they were done for the day. Forget Talented and Gifted; TAG stood for Terrified and Guilty now.

"Have a seat," Rhea said, indicating nine available balance balls. Fran and Steven exchanged an awkward glance and then carefully lowered themselves onto two white orbs. They rocked side to side and offered each other their arms to help them stabilize. Their wobbling would have been hilarious under any other circumstances, but right now they were frustrated, which meant their wrath would be even wrathier.

"Thank you for coming in on such short notice," Rhea said, handing Steven a thin stack of papers. Ruthie could see the red pen as he flipped through: 73 percent in math, 68 percent in science, and 71 percent in English.

I can't even fail at failing!

Not that Ruthie wanted to fail. Not anymore. She was desperate to stay in TAG. Desperate to stay with her only friends.

"Oh," Steven said, unbuttoning his suit jacket. "I was expecting worse."

Fran turned to face him so quickly she almost rolled onto the floor. "Really?"

"What?"

"She's never gotten below a ninety-seven."

It was really ninety-eight, but this was no time to split hairs.

"I told you she was in over her head," Fran told Steven, "and you said I was overreacting."

"I did not say *overreacting*, Fran," he said, in that lawyer voice of his. "I said we should give it more time."

"No, you specifically said *overreacting*."

"You're wrong."

"No, *you're* wrong."

Rhea cleared her throat. "Actually, I think you're both wrong," she said gently. "Ruthie isn't in over her head, and she does not need more time. She is a gifted student with a photographic memory and an infectious passion for knowledge. Ruthie does not lack ability."

Fran and Steven sat up a bit taller, their balance balls suddenly still.

"Meaning?" Fran dared.

"I suspect Ruthie performed poorly on purpose."

"On purpose?" they said together.

"I've seen this happen before, although I have to admit I never thought I'd see it from Ruthie," Rhea said with a disappointed frown. "Most kids would roll around in duck dung to be part of this program—"

"Odd visual," Steven muttered.

Rhea ignored him and continued. "But some kids don't want to be in TAG. They find it polarizing. I think your daughter purposely threw her tests for that very reason. Think about it." Then to Ruthie, "Could there be some truth to my theory?"

Ruthie paused, knowing that what she was about

to say might not bode well for her mother. But she was tired of lies and cover-ups. Regardless of how they were intended, they caused more anguish than the truth. And Ruthie was done with anguish. "My mom and I were talking about how hard it is for brains and hearts to be happy at the same time, and she said . . . She said to go with my heart."

"You *what*?" Steven asked.

Fran drew back her head. "Wait, how is this my fault?"

"You said if you had to choose, you'd choose your heart."

"Ruthie, we were talking about my work versus my family. So, yes, I said I'd choose you and Dad over my practice. Though I'm not clear on how that relates to your situation."

Ruthie looked down, noticed her missing friendship bracelets, and welled up with tears. To think she had been about to sacrifice her education for two people who wouldn't even sacrifice their Friday night. Could she have been any more pathetic? Needy? Self-sabotaging?

"Ruthie!" Steven barked. He was a hardened criminal lawyer. Crying meant nothing to him. "Answer your mother's question."

"What was it again?" Ruthie sniffled.

"What were you choosing?" he said. "What was more important than your education?"

"My friends," she peeped.

"Friends?"

"Drew and Fonda?" asked Fran.

Ruthie nodded as tears slithered down her cheeks.

"Are you serious?" Steven asked.

"I don't feel that way anymore," Ruthie pleaded. "I want to be here now. I swear."

"Case closed," Steven said to Rhea. He stood, buttoned his suit jacket, and returned the tests to her desk. "I'm sorry to have wasted your time, Rhea."

"It's Ray-a," she said. "And I have recommended that Ruthie be transferred into regular classes. We want our students to be happy, and if she's not happy—"

Ruthie stood. "But I was happy. I mean I *am* happy. I want to stay."

Rhea began stuffing papers in her tote. The conversation was over. "Ruthie, TAG is a special program that only works if we have students who *really* want to be here. I think the best thing for you to do is give the general curriculum a try, and if you keep your grades up, we can revisit the topic next year." Then to the Goldmans: "Thank you for coming in. I hope your daughter finds what she's looking for. She was a pleasure."

With that, Rhea was gone, leaving Ruthie in the classroom with two indignant parents and the first academic problem she didn't know how to solve.

chapter twenty-four.

AFTER SCHOOL ON Monday, Doug flopped down on the couch beside Drew and turned on the TV. He smelled like sunscreen and surf. At least one of them had a life.

"You can't watch on a school night," she reminded him. Not because she was a stickler for the family rules, but because she wanted to sulk alone.

"Mom and Dad are on a hike. We've got an hour." He clicked through the channels and settled on a documentary about war veterans.

While Doug watched, Drew relived the horrors of her day.

1. Seeing Ruthie leave thirty minutes early so they wouldn't have to walk to school together

2. Drew and Fonda walking on opposite sides of the street so they wouldn't have to walk to school together

3. Pretending not to notice that Fonda was on the opposite side of the street

4. Pretending not to notice Fonda sitting beside her in four classes

5. Eating lunch alone in the library

6. Getting kicked out of the library for eating

7. Not seeing Will during lunch

8. Seeing Will and Henry skate away from her after school

9. The entire Goldman family driving by on Drew's walk home and not offering her a ride (Fonda was on the opposite side of the street when the Goldmans drove by, and they didn't offer her a ride either. Which helped.)

10. Knowing that her ex–best friends were next door and she couldn't talk to them

In the documentary, one of the veterans, a guy named Mo, tragically lost his leg and was describing his phantom pains.

"What are those?" Drew asked Doug.

"It's real pain he feels in the place where his leg used to be."

Had this been last week, Drew would have wondered how a missing body part could cause physical pain, since it was no longer there. But now she understood. Though all her limbs were intact, Drew could still feel Fonda and Ruthie inside her body, even though they were gone for good. It was the worst kind of pain she'd ever known.

"I know what happened with your friends," Doug said, eyes fixed on the screen.

"How?"

"Instagram."

"Great," Drew said. She reached for the knife in her brother's bowl and handed it to him. "Help me out and get these bracelets off my arm."

"All of them?" Doug asked. "You sure?"

"Cut."

Doug lifted his leg and cut a fart.

"Ew!" Drew whacked his butt with a pillow.

"What?" He laughed. "You said you were sure."

She held out her arm again. "Cut these instead."

He sliced through all eight strings and caught the falling beads in an empty bowl. Drew's stomach lurched. Ugh, why had she lied? She should have given Ruthie and Fonda another chance to be supportive. She should have trusted them more.

"I can't believe this is happening," she cried, no longer able to pretend she was okay. "Ruthie is mad at me; I'm mad at Ruthie. Fonda is mad at me; I'm mad at Fonda. I'm also mad at myself because—"

"Silence!" Doug insisted, then farted again. "Girl stuff is for Mom, remember. Give me the boy stuff."

Drew rolled onto her side, hugged a pillow into her chest, and told him all about her night with Will. Everything from their sunset skate to the Henry-dibs scandal, the L-word exchange, and how Ruthie ruined it all.

"Yeah, I saw that on the video. Did you really say if Will was hurt, you wouldn't help him?" Doug asked.

"Technically, yes, but—"

"You won't get into a good nursing college with an attitude like that."

"I'm not worried about college applications right now; I'm worried about Will."

Doug clenched his teeth like the grimace emoji and shuddered. "For good reason. The entire party shouted 'diss!' at him, *and* the moment went viral. That's tough to bounce back from."

Drew kicked his thigh. "Don't make me feel worse."

"Sorry." Doug turned off the TV and got serious. "Have you talked to him since?"

"No. He ran out of the party and avoided me all day."

"What are you going to do?"

"Tell him I'm sorry?"

"No," Doug said. "Don't *tell* him you're sorry. Show him."

♥

AFTER DINNER, DREW found Will's address in the school directory and begged Doug for a ride.

"Wait for me down the street," she said.

"Why not here?"

"I don't want you to watch me."

"Why not?"

"It's embarrassing."

"Young love often is," he teased before driving off. Leaving her to trespass on her crush's property at eight thirty at night, surrounded by garden gnomes that may or may not have been ironic, with a laptop in one hand and a Nerf football in the other.

Drew quietly circled the house in search of Will's bedroom and found it in the back overlooking the pool. He had a pool! The curtains were blue, the wall was covered in skate posters, and the bed was unmade. *Total Will,* she thought. Then she prayed he'd appear in the next ten minutes, because her parents wanted them home no later than nine.

Drew finally spotted him around minute eight and chucked the ball at his window. He peered outside, then disappeared from view. She retrieved the football and chucked it again. Then again. And again. And again. And again. And again. And again. And again. And again. And again. And again. And again. And again. And again. And again. And again. And again.

And again. And again. And again. And again. And again. And again. And again.

Finally, he slid open the window and shouted, "Dude!"

With shaky hands, Drew lifted the laptop over her head and played a clip from *The Skateboard Kid*. It was the scene where Rip the skateboard gets hit by lightning and comes to life. "I'm back," he tells Zack Tyler. "And I'm on a roll."

Drew was sure it would make him laugh. Or at the very least make him want to hear her out.

Except it didn't.

Will slammed his window shut before the scene was over. At first, Drew thought he was running outside to accept her apology. So she laid her laptop on the grass, tightened her ponytail, and dried her clammy hands on her sweatpants. Then she waited . . . and waited . . . and waited . . . But Will never came down.

chapter twenty-five.

AVA H. PUSHED her organic turkey wrap aside and leaned forward. "So . . ." she began in that I'm-about-to-spill-some-extremely-hot-tea sort of way. Fonda was at the Avas' table in the Lunch Garden for the second day in a row, laying claim to their fourth seat.

"What kind of name is Fonda? Norwegian?"

"No, it's feminist. My mom has a thing for strong women. My sisters are Winfrey as in Oprah and Amelia as in Earhart. I'm Fonda as in Jane."

"Pause," said Ava G. "Who's Fonda Jane?"

"It's Jane Fonda, actually."

"The one who saves chimpanzees?"

"No, that's Jane Goodall," said Ava H., with a bat

of her eyelash extensions. "Jane Fonda is that tall chick who played Sue Sylvester on *Glee*."

"That was Jane Lynch," said Fonda, knowing Drew and Ruthie would be poking each other under the table if they heard this nonsense. Especially since the Avas, like the Janes, shared a name and should be more sensitive to this type of confusion. "Jane Fonda is a civil rights activist who has spoken out against the Vietnam War and climate change. She also won a ton of awards for acting."

But it wasn't Jane they were interested in. It was Fonda. Fonda Miller, the seventh-grade star of the most viewed party post ever. She was also the queen bee of irony. Because when a girl who was desperate to matter finally started to matter only to hate it, ironic was the perfect way to describe it. Other than annoying. Which it definitely was.

Every hallway, classroom, bathroom, sidewalk, and Starbucks that Fonda had frequented since Friday night became an opportunity for someone to say, "Epic PP," or "You got soooo busted."

The attention felt good at first. It put Fonda on the

party map, associated her with the Avas, and let everyone know that as a friend, she was available.

Except she wasn't. Not in her heart, anyway.

Explaining her name to a new group of girls was tedious. Decoding their inside jokes was draining. And pretending she was someone she wasn't—a period-having, good-humored PP star—was exhausting. Hanging out with Ruthie and Drew had always been so easy and effortless, the way it was supposed to be with true best friends. But Ruthie had made it clear that their friendship was over. And Drew hadn't looked at her since Friday.

Fonda packed up her uneaten sandwich. Was this really it? Were they really over? She consulted the Magic 8 Ball in her gut. It said, *All signs point to yes.* In English, Fonda noticed that Drew had cut off her friendship bracelets. When she spotted Ruthie in the halls between classes and asked what she was doing there, Ruthie took off. But were they really done? Was Fonda an Ava? It was something she'd wanted for so long, and now that it was happening, the whole thing felt awkward. Like she was wearing someone else's flip-flops and the fit was off. The rubber was worn in unusual places, and the toe prints weren't hers. Seasonal and temporary, they were good in a pinch. But Fonda wanted something permanent. Something that was built to last.

Ava R. waved a hand in front of Fonda's face. "Hel-loooo! Are you even listening?"

"Yeah, sorry. Something about hair?"

"I was asking when you started using a curling iron."

Fonda felt the back of her head. The smoothness was gone. In its place were bumpy, wild curls. "This is my natural texture. I didn't straighten it this morning."

"Oh, poo." Ava G. pouted. "We liked it the non-natural way." She tucked a sleek strand of her own straight hair behind her ear, revealing a stain of left-over gold paint by her temple.

"Guess what?" said Ava R. "I totally CC'd in science today. First one of the year!"

They exchanged a round of high fives, which Fonda did not participate in because, once again, she had zero idea what they were talking about.

"What made you do it?" asked Ava G.

"We were dissecting frogs, and I couldn't deal."

Fonda let them go on a bit longer, hoping that, in time, they'd reveal the meaning of CC, because she was dead tired of asking what everything meant. But she cracked.

"What's CC?"

"Calling cramps," said Ava R. "You do it to get out of a situation you don't want to be in."

Fonda shrugged. She still didn't get it.

"Period cramps."

"Yeah, I still don't—"

"It's the excuse you give when you don't want to participate."

"It works super well with male teachers," added Ava H. "Trust me. They do not want to challenge you on something like that."

Fonda wished she could call cramps on the entire school year and go back to the way things were. She missed Drew and Ruthie. They were her solid, comfortable shoes. A perfect fit.

♥

THE REST OF the afternoon was spent strategizing. Instead of listening in class, Fonda filled pages of her notebooks with corny apology poems and elaborate schemes to win back her friends. But it wasn't until last period, while everyone was changing for PE, that she settled on a plan.

"Coach Pierce," Fonda mewled, clutching her abdomen.

He spit the whistle from his mouth. "Don't tell me you forgot your uniform."

"No, I have it. It's just that—" She scrunched up her face the way women in labor do in the movies. "I don't think I can run today."

The coach crossed his hands over his Santa belly. "And why not?"

"Cramps."

He squinted at her, as if he had X-ray vision and could read brains.

Fonda scrunched up her face again.

"Fine," he sighed. "Go." He gave her a slip and sent her to the nurse's office, but Fonda walked straight out of Poplar Middle School's front doors instead.

Back in sixth grade, Joan had filed a letter with the principal giving her daughter permission to leave campus whenever she wanted. "If you want to cut class and flunk out, go for it," she had said. "This is your education, not mine. No one should care more about it than you."

Fonda had never taken advantage of the letter and swore she never would. But desperate times called for desperate measures. And Fonda was desperate to get her nesties back.

♥

AT THREE FORTY-FIVE P.M., Fonda was in position on her front lawn, seated in a beach chair with a gift bag on either side. Nervous her plan would fail, she lifted her face to the sun to absorb its optimism. Three black crows were hanging out on the wire overhead.

Nesties, she thought. It was a good sign.

Just then, Drew and Ruthie appeared (on opposite sides of the street) and hurried for their houses.

Fonda stood and called, "Wait!"

The crows took off. The girls kept walking.

"Can we please talk?"

As they approached their front doors, Fonda shouted, "Stop!" They did, but neither girl turned around to face her.

"That's fine. You don't have to look at me, just don't leave."

Fonda took a deep, steadying breath. She had spoken to Drew and Ruthie a trillion times in her life, and never once had her hands been so shaky, her throat so tight. What if it was too late for forgiveness? What if they never wanted to talk to her again? What if the only friends who mattered to Fonda decided that she no longer mattered to *them*?

"I'm going to say a few things," she began, "and all you have to do is listen. If you like something I say, maybe you can take a step toward me. And if you don't, I dunno, stay where you are, I guess."

They remained still.

Fonda looked up at the sun one last time. *You've got this*, it seemed to say.

"The last three days without you have been the worst. I sat with the Avas at lunch, and all I could think was, 'I'd rather eat with Drew on the lawn and miss Ruthie than sit with them.' Not because they're mean or anything, but because they're not us."

The girls didn't move.

"I'm sorry," she continued. "I did some really

terrible things to both of you." She paused, giving them time to turn around, maybe take a step. They didn't. "Not just by lying. I mean, yeah, that was the *most* terrible, but I did other terrible things."

Still nothing.

"I wanted the Avas to notice me so badly, like I was a seed or something and their noticing would make me grow into some awesome flower that everyone would want to take selfies with."

"What does that even mean?" Ruthie said to her front door.

"Bad analogy. What I meant was, they finally noticed me, and it didn't make me happy. It didn't solve my problems, and it didn't make me feel like I belonged. It made me feel like a lonely dumb-dumb who should have known I *belong* with you guys."

Drew and Ruthie turned around.

Fonda's throat unlocked a little.

"We were perfect the way we were, and I wanted to change that. Why? To impress a bunch of strangers. It was pathetic and desperate and a total waste, because you're the only people I care about impressing."

Ruthie took a step.

"Ruthie, I'm so proud to have a genius friend with a chic French haircut who isn't afraid to be exactly who she is."

Step.

"I shouldn't have tried to make you act like me or Drew or anyone else, because the thing I love about you most is that you're nothing like us. You're a pale-skinned unicorn that poops fro-yo and sneezes puzzle pieces. And I don't ever want that to change."

Step.

"I don't even care that you called me a dumb-dumb, because I was a dumb-dumb. The dumb-dumbest!"

Step. Step.

"I should have told you I was invited to that party and I should have asked if we could switch the Spatacular to the next night. If that made you feel bad, we could have talked about it. But I never gave you that chance, and I wish I did."

Step. Step.

Ruthie was close enough now that Fonda could see the rainbows on her socks. "And if I ever get invited to another party again, I'll only say yes if you're both invited too, or I'm not breaking plans we already have."

Step.

Arms.

Torso.

Hug!

Fonda's entire body felt warm and melty as she breathed in Ruthie's familiar strawberry-scented shampoo. It was that same sense of relief she experienced when she changed into sweats after school. Like the trying was over and she could finally relax.

"I like your hair better this way," Ruthie said when they pulled apart. "You may not think the curls are fancy, but they feel right. Oh, and I'm sorry I said 'you put the *end* in *friend*.'"

"Don't be." Fonda smiled. "It was a five-star line."

Ruthie grinned. "It was, wasn't it?"

"Big-time."

They hugged again, and suddenly, all was right in the world.

Almost.

Drew was still standing by her front door like a kid whose mother forgot to pick her up from school.

"I'm sorry I didn't believe you when you said Will must have had a reason for being weird. He obviously did have a reason, or you wouldn't have gone to the party with him, right?"

Drew stepped forward.

"And I assume you found out what that reason was."

She stepped forward again.

"And I assume if you ever forgive me, you'll tell me what that reason is, right?"

"If you stop saying reason," Drew said, then quickly covered her mouth.

"I will stop saying reason."

Step.

A zap of excitement shot up Fonda's spine. Underneath all the hurt and resentment, they were still very much them. "I was only anti-Will because he was acting weird, which was making you act weird, and I thought you deserved better. I was trying to look out for you. That's all."

Drew stepped forward, but Fonda wanted her even closer. She wanted to see that scar between her lip and left nostril, the one she got from walking into a tree branch when they were nine and playing blindfold tag.

"I never should have claimed bad chicken to go to a party, and I shouldn't have made you feel like *you* had to claim bad chicken to go on a skate hang. And the next time you go on one of those, tell me. I'll help you put on your helmet."

Drew took two giant steps forward and stopped by the back bumper of her mother's Subaru. Four more and Fonda would have eyes on that scar.

"You're a great catch who isn't afraid to wear protective pads to a party."

Step.

"And Will must be great too, because he thought it was funny."

Step.

"You're seriously crushable and will probably get asked on a ton of skate hangs this year. And I want to be there to take your picture and hug you before you go."

Step.

"And I want to get the gossip when you get back."

Step.

Scar.

Arms.

Torso.

Hug!

"I'm sorry I claimed bad chicken. I should have told you both the truth," Drew said as Ruthie joined their hug. "I was embarrassed that I liked Will even though you thought I shouldn't. I'm also sorry I ignored the color-of-the-day thing. I was just so over uniforms, and—"

"It's okay," Fonda said, "I get it. I never should have told you what to wear. But you know what I'm most sorry about?"

The girls shook their heads.

"That I lost four days of hanging out with you."

When they hugged again, Fonda caught a glimpse of that telephone wire and smiled. The three crows were back.

"Starting now, I want to hear everything about TAG and Will. Ev-er-y-thing! Don't leave one thing out—"

Drew's posture wilted. "Will won't talk to me."

"And I got kicked out of TAG."

"What?" Fonda gasped. "Is that why I saw you in the halls?"

Ruthie nodded. She was suddenly too choked up to speak.

"Well, we're going to fix this," Fonda promised.

"How?" Drew asked.

Fonda clapped *no clue* in Morse code, which cracked them up. Then, "Wait, I have gifts!"

She handed them each a bag and proudly watched as they dug past the tissue paper and pulled out their white-and-red polka-dotted period purses.

"Thanks," Ruthie said politely. "But we don't have our periods yet."

"Open it," Fonda said.

They pulled back the zippers, probably expecting to find Ziplocs and underwear, maxi pads, baby wipes, and Reece's Pieces, but Fonda was no dumb-dumb. Not anymore.

"New friendship bracelets!" Drew gasped.

"Where did you make these?' Ruthie asked, admiring the strand of gold beads.

"I cut PE and went to the Gem House."

"Gotta love that letter from Joan," said Drew. Then she glanced at Fonda's bare wrist. "Where's yours?"

Fonda reached into the pocket of her jeans, pulled out her matching bracelet, and slipped it on. The other girls did the same.

"So, we're good?"

"We're good," they said.

Then they put their arms around each other and fell to the grass, just like they had in the picture on Fonda's vision board. Only this time, they were not going to let anyone or anything rip them apart.

chapter twenty-six.

RUTHIE AND HER parents had been strolling through town eating a post-dinner gelato and enjoying the ocean-scented evening. But rather than admiring the art galleries and applauding the street performers, Ruthie was mining the last bits of cinnamon swirl from her cup, hoping to make the treat last as long as possible. Because the moment that cup hit the trash can, something bad was going to happen. It always did.

During their last post-dinner gelato, Ruthie was told her dog had to be put to sleep. Before that, Grandpa Stu had a heart attack. And before that, Grumpy Cat died.

"Is that a new bracelet?" Fran had asked, lifting a spoonful of mango to her mouth.

"Yeah, Fonda gave it to me after school yesterday."

"I like the gold."

"Same."

"So everyone's friends again?"

"Yeah," Ruthie said, her answer short on purpose. As much as she wanted to avoid the news, she wanted to get it already. Anticipation gave her gas.

"And what about Drew?" her father asked.

"We're good."

Fran and Steven exchanged one of their looks. Ruthie couldn't take it anymore. She tossed her cup. It was time.

"Guess what?" Fran said.

Here it comes . . .

"Dad and I heard about an amazing new TAG charter school in San Clemente called Expansions and—"

"San Clemente?" Ruthie cried. "Mom, I don't want to switch schools."

"Well, you can't stay at Poplar," Steven said.

"Why not?"

"We think it's a bad influence on you."

Ruthie didn't have to be talented or gifted to understand what was happening. "Throwing the test scores was *my* idea, I swear! Fonda and Drew didn't know anything about it. If I told them, they never would have let me do it."

"That doesn't change the fact that you won't be challenged by a standard curriculum."

Her mother was right. Ruthie had spent the last two days in regular classes and memorized the first chapter of *The Outsiders* to stay awake. Her brain would melt if she had to sit through material she already knew. But her heart would melt if she had to leave her friends all over again. Tears rushed to her eyes. See? She was melting already.

"Let's focus on solutions," Steven said. "Your mother and I think switching to Expansions is a great one. If you have another suggestion, we're open to it. What we're not open to is keeping you in a program that stunts your growth."

"What if I can get back into TAG?"

Steven mussed her hair. "Then you're a better litigator than I am, kid."

♥

RUTHIE STAYED UP all night poring over her father's law books, searching for a precedent that would make it illegal for Rhea to base her decision on one—albeit one major—misstep. At two o'clock in the morning, her resolve was getting sleepy. She wanted to throw a rock at Fonda's window and wake her up. Remind her that she promised to help her figure this out and hold her to it. Then she realized Fonda had already helped.

Her apology yesterday hadn't been full of legal jargon or hard-hitting facts on why she should be forgiven. It was sincere and apologetic. It showed accountability and made a case for forgiveness. It spoke not to the judge but to the jury. Not to the brain, but to the heart.

Ruthie spent the next few hours working on an essay to Rhea called "TAG: Titans Are Guilty." It was about Zeus, who banished his fellow deities to Tartarus, which was extremely cruel and beyond harsh. She proposed rewriting Titan history and not banishing anyone. Instead, give Titans a chance to right their wrongs. Because everyone, no matter how smart they are, should be allowed to make mistakes. How else will they learn to fix them?

Beeeeeep. Beeeep. Beeeep.

Ruthie's alarm clock began to sound. It was six

forty-five A.M. Had she slept at all, it would have been time to get up. Instead, she blew a good-luck kiss at her computer screen and sent the essay to Rhea. Then she took a shower and checked her inbox. Nothing. She got dressed and checked again. Nothing. She ate breakfast. Nothing. Brushed her teeth. Nothing. Said goodbye to Foxie. Nothing. Kicked the leg of her desk. Nothing.

Eyes burning and toe throbbing, Ruthie walked to school with Drew and Fonda, wishing she could be as excited as they were to be in class together. But everything was different now. Ruthie had a new kind of faith in their bond and trusted that they'd still be nesties, whether they shared a lunch period or not. Their fight, or rather, their apology, gave Ruthie a sense of security with the girls she'd never known she needed. They weren't going to move on without her. They didn't *want* to. She could feed her heart and her brain, and they would support her in that. Celebrate her for it, even. But it wasn't up to Drew and Fonda anymore. It was up to Rhea, who still hadn't acknowledged Ruthie's essay when the first-period bell rang.

As Ruthie shyly settled into biology (still without

Drew or Fonda!) and tried to adjust to the hard bottom of the wood seat, Principal Bell poked her head in the room and said, "Miss Goldman, grab your things and come with me."

Ruthie quickly stood. The room spun. "Are my parents okay?"

"Everyone is fine," she said as they hurried down the empty hall.

"Then what is it?"

"You're late for class."

"But—"

She handed Ruthie a late slip. Beside the room number, it said *TAG*. "Hurry."

Ruthie hugged the woman, twice, and then ran.

"Welcome home!" said Rhea as Ruthie entered the classroom, her smile wide and forgiving.

Sage grinned at her, and Tomoyo and Everest flashed her the thumbs-up. Ruthie found her balance ball and sat without the slightest wobble. She was back!

"Titans," Rhea said, her tone now grave, "one should never be judged for their mistakes, but rather, what they do to correct them. Now, class, tell me: Titans Are—"

Ruthie waved her hand high in the air. "Grateful. Titans Are Grateful."

Rhea smiled wide. "Indeed."

The rest of the day flew by, and when Ruthie left her classroom with Sage, Drew and Fonda were waiting for her.

"We heard you got back in!" Fonda said.

"Congratulations," Drew said, handing her a bran muffin. "I got it at the cafeteria. I didn't have enough money for a cupcake."

"Are you really going with those dumb-dumbs?" Sage asked.

"Of course. They're my best friends," Ruthie said proudly.

Sage lowered her chin and peered at them over the black frames of her glasses. "Seriously?"

Ruthie was shocked. She liked Sage and believed they could become legitimate friends. She also loved her nesties and didn't want to lose them again. But Sage would always think they were dummies and they would always think she was a snob unless she found a way to bring the two worlds together.

"Drew and Fonda aren't dumb-dumbs," Ruthie told

Sage. "They are the smartest people I've ever met. And you're not a dummy either."

"Who said I was a dummy?"

"Anyone who's ever heard you call someone a dumb-dumb."

"Yeah," Fonda said. "It's a pre-K word."

"Correction," said Drew. "It's pre-pre-K. That's how dumb-dumb you are."

Sage screwed her face forward, ready to launch a full verbal strike.

"Stop using the D-word!" Ruthie said. "No one here is a D. I would never be friends with Ds."

Sage scoffed.

"I'll prove it."

"Yay! A spelling bee!"

"No, Sage," Ruthie said. "An invitation. Hang out with us on Sunday." She didn't dare make eye contact with Fonda and Drew, because they were probably death-glaring her. And this was not a situation Ruthie wanted to back down from. She was a Titan, after all. And Titans Are Gutsy.

"Really?" Sage asked, more suspicious than flattered.

"Yes, really."

"How do you guys feel about frozen yogurt?"

"It's fine," Drew said, clearly trying to play it cool.

"Will there be toppings?" Fonda asked.

"Unlimited."

"I like toppings," Fonda said cautiously.

"Great. Because I have a gift card to Fresh & Fruity. I got it for my birthday last year, and it's about to expire. It has just enough to cover four mediums."

"Why haven't you used it yet?" Drew asked, warming.

"It's no fun going alone."

And for the first time ever, they all agreed.

chapter twenty-seven.

DREW DID A spontaneous cartwheel during their walk home from school that day. No, Will hadn't forgiven her, but it didn't matter. She had two other reasons to feel happy; they were both walking beside her wearing matching bead bracelets and chitchatting about their days. Sometimes that was all it took.

"See?" Ruthie said. "Sage isn't so bad."

"No one ever is once you get to know them," Fonda said in that mocking tone she used to imitate her mother.

"Except Will," Drew said, surprising herself. It had been three days since her big apology, and she had told herself she was over him. But her feelings for him were like burps—unexpected bubbles that welled up inside her that had to be released. Once they were, she felt better and could move on. Was she still a little nervous Will-burping out loud? Yes, but so far Fonda had stayed true to her word. She didn't judge Drew or try to solve anything. She simply listened and acted sad in all the right places. "I can't believe he shut down my apology like that."

"Recap," Fonda said. "You apologized, and he slammed the window in your face?"

"Pretty much, yeah."

"Pretty much?"

"Well, I didn't actually say 'I'm sorry,' but—"

"So, you never actually apologized?" Ruthie asked.

"I think going to his house and throwing a Nerf football at his window for fifteen minutes and then playing a scene from *The Skateboard Kid* counts as an apology."

They looked at her like they weren't so sure it did.

"Oh my dog, look—" Ruthie shouted. She was pointing at a boy lying on the curb across the street, his skateboard rolling down the sidewalk.

Will!

And he was injured!

Drew's heart began to gallop. Her hands began to shake. She had to help him!

"Coming!" She looked both ways and darted across Fontana Avenue.

Now, as she stood above him, Will waved her away like a smelly sock. "I'm fine."

"Says you. But I need to rule out a spine injury. Can you wiggle your toes?"

"I said I'm fine," Will insisted, straining to sit. "I just scraped my back."

"I'll be the judge of that." She crouched down behind him and slowly, carefully, lifted him upright. "Why weren't you wearing a helmet?"

"On my back?"

Drew laughed at the visual. "It wouldn't be the worst idea. You really are accident-prone." Then, returning to her nurse voice, said, "Would you mind lifting up your shirt so I can take a look?"

"Seriously?"

"Seriously."

Will reached back, grabbed the bottom of his shirt, and winced.

"Looks like you hurt your arm too."

He groaned.

Upon investigation, Drew concluded that he had a minor abrasion. He had lost about one cc of blood, which wasn't enough to cause dizziness or warrant a transfusion, but the wound did need to be cleaned and sealed. But how?

Drew searched her backpack for a napkin or a tissue, but all she found was a binder, her dirty PE uniform, one bran muffin, and the period purse Fonda gave her, which she was using as a pencil case.

Period purse!

"Fonda!" Drew called urgently. "I need you. STAT!"

Fonda and Ruthie raced to her side, sleeves rolled and ready to help.

"Do you have your period purse?"

Without hesitating, Fonda dug inside her backpack and slapped it into Drew's open hand.

"Do you need any essential oils?" Fonda asked.

"No."

"Reece's Pieces?"

"Yes," Drew said, opening her mouth so Fonda could drop a few in.

"You guys," Will said. "I'm *fine*."

"Sir, try to relax," Drew said. "You've lost a lot of blood. You're not thinking clearly."

"Sir?" He chuckled. "What is happening here?"

Ignoring him, Drew opened the purse, and as she had hoped, there was a giant maxi pad inside. She held the sanitary cotton slab against his scrape, pressed the sticky strip against his shirt, and applied direct pressure to the wound.

"I think I'm good," Will said, standing.

"You got it?" Drew asked, taking his arm and directing it toward the pad. "Keep holding it until you get home."

"Whatever," he said, limping toward his board.

"Will!" Drew called.

He turned around like an arthritic grandfather.

"I'm sorry," Drew said.

"For what?"

"Saying I wouldn't cross the road for you. I would. I *did*!"

His sparkly smile returned. "Yeah. I guess you did. Thanks."

Will didn't reach for her hand. He didn't compliment Drew on her grace under pressure. But he was looking at her the way he did on Ava G.'s back porch, and that was even better. It meant that the story between Drew and the boy with a maxi pad on his back wasn't over. That maybe it was just getting stah-ted.

chapter twenty-eight.

"WAIT," WINFREY SAID. "He really walked down the street with a maxi pad stuck to his back?" She couldn't get enough of the story, and neither could Amelia. Why else would they be in the living room, sharing a pizza with Fonda, Drew, and Ruthie on a Friday night? They had outfits to plan, parties to attend, hearts to break.

"Hey," Amelia said, reaching for her third slice. "What did the pad say to the fart?"

"Dunno," said the girls.

"You are the wind beneath my wings."

"What is Will's favorite food?" Winfrey asked. "*Pad Thai noodles!*"

Fonda laughed so hard she almost choked on a mushroom. "What did Will's mom say when he stayed out past curfew?" she asked. "You've been a paaaad boy."

"What's Will's favorite movie?" Ruthie asked. "*Paddington.*"

"Come on, guys, stop," Drew said. "I feel pad for him."

Fonda thought she was going to puke laughter right there on the shag rug. Instead, she felt a little trickle of wetness leak out of her body and into her underwear.

It was happening. Her period was actually happening! She'd heard that being near an active menstruator might trigger her flow, but who knew talking about maxi pads would have the same effect?

"Be right back!" Fonda announced as she hurried to the bathroom, her last trip as a girl. When she emerged, she'd be a woman, worthy of facials by Katrine, snickerdoodles for dinner, and her sisters' secrets. Her mother would teach her how to use a tampon, and next time she hung out with the Avas, she could claim cramps for real!

Door locked and bright lights on, Fonda untied her sweatpants, then paused to commemorate her final moment as a child. She took three deep breaths and, on the fourth, pulled down her pants and—

"Huh?" Her underwear was a teeny-bit wet, except the wet wasn't red. *Was that even possible?* Fonda performed an investigatory wipe; all she saw was a faint trace of yellow.

As it happened, the trickle of blood she'd felt was really a trickle of joy, because sometimes joy made her pee a little.

Had the false alarm happened last month, last week, or even yesterday, Fonda would have shamed her body for being too slow to join the P club. Today all she did was wash her hands and fluff her curls. It was hardly the opportunity she had in mind, but it was golden nonetheless.

The next morning, after everyone went home, Fonda pulled the vision board out from under her bed and began tearing off the pictures. She pulled off the fancy outfits, the red circle, Poplar Middle, and even the fortune she had taped to the top.

The only image she kept was of her, Drew, and Ruthie laughing on the grass, because it was the only one that mattered.

Period.

acknowledgments.

If you made it this far, that means:

A) You genuinely enjoyed reading *Girl Stuff* and don't want it to end.
B) You're grounded or sheltering in place and are super bored.
C) The Wi-Fi is down.
D) You contributed to this novel and are wondering if I had the decency to thank you.

Regardless of the reason, I'm happy you're here. It's important to acknowledge the brilliant people who help me turn half-baked ideas into books. If not for them, you'd be reading a stack of tearstained Post-it Notes.

Jennifer Klonsky, president and publisher at Putnam Young Readers, is the North Star and champion of this series. Her vision was unwavering, and her sense of humor is next-level. We're talking zero fake laughs when she's in the room. Zeeeero.

Thank you, Jen Loja, president of Penguin Young Readers, for your endless support.

My friends and longtime collaborators at Alloy Entertainment also deserve top billing. Josh Bank, Sara Shandler, and Lanie Davis—you are the best in the biz. Your genius and guidance are invaluable; the laughter is a calorie-burner. My love and gratitude run deep.

Thank you to the deal makers: Richard Abate, my badass agent, shrink, and confidant of eighteen years. FUMP. James Gregorio, my velvet-voiced lawyer. And Romy Golan, for getting these books into foreign countries and making it seem like I can write in multiple languages.

Thank you, Olivia Russo, Christina Colangelo, Kara Brammer, Carmela Iaria, and Alex Garber, for your PR and marketing genius. You are why this novel has been read.

Thank you, Jessica Jenkins and Judit Mallol, for

this fabulous cover. Thank you, Suki Boynton, for making the inside look equally fabulous. Copyeditors Ana Deboo, Jacqueline Hornberger, and Cindy Howle probably had you thinking I aced grammar in school. I didn't. They did.

Thank you, Caitlin Tutterow, for making it all run so smoothly.

Thank you, JJ Hutcheon, for always weighing in when I need you. Thank you to the middle school girls in my Laguna Beach Clique Club. You inspire me every day, and I am wildly honored to know you.

Lastly, thank you to the voices in my head. Thirty-five books later, and you're still showing up. Don't ever stop.

Xoxo Lisi

THERE'S ALWAYS MORE GIRL STUFF!

Fonda, Drew, and Ruthie are on
a mission to make sure their seventh-grade
field trip is the best ever, but everything's getting
in their way—including their hearts.